He caught her in the dark . . .

"Let me go, Steve, you hateful beast!" she spat at him. "You've just told me to keep out of your business, so kindly do the same with mine."

"And let you injure yourself? Nicole, sometimes you are such a child!"

"Am I, indeed?" She stopped struggling, stung into action by his insult. Her hands slid up to his shoulders and then touched his face, and her body eased and curled itself into his, hips molded to his thighs. What she was doing was foolish and provocative, she knew, but more than anger was directing her now.

He let her go almost as roughly as he had seized her.

"Oh, no, you don't!" he said contemptuously. "That may be your favorite weapon whenever you need to score a point, to get your own way, but you aren't going to use it on me again. If I *did* want to make love to you, it wouldn't be under those conditions."

Lee Stafford was born and educated in Sheffield where she worked as a secretary and in public relations. Her husband is in hospital catering management. They live in Sussex with their two teenage daughters.

Yesterday's Enemy
Lee Stafford

Harlequin Books

TORONTO • NEW YORK • LONDON
AMSTERDAM • PARIS • SYDNEY • HAMBURG
STOCKHOLM • ATHENS • TOKYO • MILAN

Original hardcover edition published in 1988
by Mills & Boon Limited

ISBN 0-373-02963-2

Harlequin Romance first edition February 1989

CHAPTER ONE

NICOLE leaned over the parapet of the roof terrace and breathed a sigh of delight at the panorama spread out beneath her. Ten years had passed since she was last here, but nothing seemed to have changed in the little Catalan fishing village of Puerto de Castello. The white houses still jumbled around the perfect horseshoe of the bay and climbed the hill haphazardly, reflecting themselves in the limpid blue of the Mediterranean. She gazed down at a jigsaw pattern of narrow streets, red-tiled rooftops and tiny, secretive gardens, punctuated by the white *campanile* of the church and the jetty of the small harbour, and knew, in spite of her earlier reluctance to return, a deep contentment at being here again.

For a moment or two, back at Vistamar, she had been convinced that her instincts had been right, and this was all a terrible mistake. As she had turned the car up the drive and caught her first glimpse of the gracious, two-storeyed white house built in the classical Hispanic style, with its ornate, iron-grilled balconies and the vast terrace full of cane outdoor furniture, a wave of nostalgia had threatened to engulf her. Her throat had felt tight and painful and, instead of a self-contained young woman of twenty-four, she had been a confused and helpless fourteen-year-old again, waiting fearfully to be turned out of the place which had been her home for three wonderful, idyllic summers. Waiting for Steve Rodriguez to come strolling up the drive, unable to contain himself decently until they had left before taking possession, rubbing salt in the wounds of the man he had ruined—her mother's beloved Teddy.

'Right, then. Here we are.' Nicole had wrenched herself forcibly back to the present, relieved that all she had to do was to unload Lacey and get the hell out. Briefly, she'd reflected on the ironic chain of coincidence which had brought her here with Steve's fourteen-year-old daughter.

A chance sharing of tables in the bar of her Paris hotel had got her into conversation with Sonia, Steve's American ex-wife, and before she knew it, Nicole had been persuaded that it would be just great if she could give Lacey a 'lift' to her father's villa, where she was to spend the summer.

'After all, honey,' argued Sonia, 'it's hardly out of your way, when you're going to the same village. I'm meeting friends in Venice, and I'm already behind schedule.'

Nicole had hesitated, doubtful about the morality of taking responsibility for the child of someone she scarcely knew.

'I'm not driving directly to Spain,' she had demurred. 'I work for a company which organises camping holidays, and I have to stop off at our sites in the Loire valley and the Dordogne to sort out any problems there may be.'

'Camping—great, Lacey will love it,' Sonia had promised confidently. 'She'll be no trouble at all.'

Nicole had admitted defeat gracefully. But three days and several hundred miles later, she had regretted the quixotic impulse which had made her give in to Sonia's cajolery, but her responsibility had ended here, and she need never see any member of the Rodriguez family again. If she could just escape without having to meet *him* . . .

She had said nothing to Sonia about her unhappy memories of the American woman's ex-husband, and, so far as Lacey knew, Nicole had never set eyes on Vistamar before in her life. But she had not needed her mother's grim admonition to keep out of *that man*'s way at all costs. Her stepfather, Teddy Walton, had died a broken man—in every way—three years earlier, and Nicole had been nurtured with her mother's hatred and bitterness towards the man whom she blamed for this.

'He'll ruin your life, too, if he knows who you are,' Lorraine Walton had said darkly. 'Never forget that for men like Steve Rodriguez it's no more than sport.'

'There's nothing he can do to me,' Nicole had soothed her. 'Our paths need never cross—I shall be in Spain to do my job, nothing more.'

But Teddy had been blithely 'doing his job,' running an import/export business with his old friend Enrique, Steve's uncle, when the younger man had come breezing back from America and decided he wanted in on the deal, and by fair means or foul, Teddy had had to go. Suddenly, all Teddy's loans were called in at once, credit was no longer available to him, and wherever he turned, every avenue was closed. With terrifying swiftness, their income and their home had gone. Nicole shook off the dark shadow of apprehension by consoling herself that, unlike poor Teddy, *she* had nothing that Esteban Rodriguez wanted.

Even if they were to meet, Nicola had very few qualms that he would recognise her. He had probably given little thought to Teddy's scrawny, nondescript teenage stepdaughter on the few occasions when they had briefly met. She had been only 'young Nicky', thin, plain and painfully shy, and the assertively dangerous young man had spared her no more than a passing glance.

Without vanity, Nicole knew she had changed some. The coltish gawkiness had filled out to a long-limbed slenderness of form, the untidy plaits were now a sleek, wafer-straight fall of beige-blonde hair, and a good education leading to a responsible position with a reputable travel company had banished much of the awkward timidity. Even her name would not give her away, for there was no reason for him to know her real father's surname, which she used.

It was Nicole Bradbury, not 'young Nicky', who stood on the roof terrace of the converted fisherman's cottage she had rented, looking out over Puerto de Castello, and rediscovering her never entirely forgotten love for this peaceful spot.

'*Adios* for now,' she said aloud, with a smile. 'I'd better go and get on with my unpacking.'

Lightly humming a popular tune, she ran back down the stairs to the living-room. And froze in her tracks, horrified.

There was a man in the room. He was standing with his back to her, over by the windows which opened on to the tiny, enclosed patio, and the split second before he turned to face her seemed to stretch out to infinity, fraught with a thousand unpleasant possibilities. She was about to be robbed or attacked . . . one heard about these things all the time, but always imagined them happening to someone else. Physically, she knew she was no match for this strong-looking intruder, and no amount of equal opportunity would make her so.

Had she had time to think logically, she would have realised that he looked too casual and at ease to be a sneak thief, but her reactions were too swift to allow this thought to develop. As he turned, slowly and calmly, she pointed forcefully to the door.

'*Vaya!*' she said coldly. 'Get out!'

'And if I don't?' he said evenly. 'Will you throw me out?'

Nicole remembered that voice—deep, quiet and deceptively soft—and suddenly she was overcome by a wave of nausea as he stood there, calmly regarding her, hands thrust deep into the pockets of his immaculately cut trousers. This was no thief—at least, not in the unsubtle, opportunist, breaking-and-entering sense. This was Esteban Rodriguez, and even after ten years she would have known him anywhere.

'It's customary to knock before entering anyone's house,'

she said coldly. He had addressed her in English—the everyday, colloquial language she used herself, not the flawless but accented version often spoken by those whose mother tongue is something else. Nicole recalled, irrationally, that an English mother and a diplomat father with frequent postings to England and the United States had enabled him to grow up effortlessly bilingual.

'And so I did, but you obviously didn't hear me, and I don't have time to be coming back and forth all day bruising my knuckles on your door,' he said, with equal coldness. 'Incidentally, if that's your car outside, you'll have to shift it or it will block the street. There's a small square about fifty yards away where you can park.'

'I know, and I'll move it, just as soon as I'm allowed to finish unloading,' Nicola said pointedly.

'That's an invitation to push off if ever I heard one,' he observed, with a touch of grim amusement. 'It won't get you anywhere. I'm staying until I've found out what I need to know.'

Nicole realised guiltily that she was staring at him, and strove to alter her expression to the impersonal gaze of a distinterested stranger. He always had been a hard man to place, a hybrid, who spoke like an Englishman, and was certainly no one's idea of the exuberant, extrovert Latin. Beneath the short sleeves of his dazzlingly white shirt his arms were very brown, but his face, although tanned, was several shades lighter, and there were glints of russet in the thick, dark hair. She had thought him tall, but he was not much above average height . . . the illusion was the result of the way he was built, the ideal balance between a sinuous slimness of hip and a compactly muscular breadth of shoulder.

He exuded, as he always had, even when he was younger, an aggressive mental energy, a power tightly reined but capable of being directed to suit his own ends. It blazed out steadily from those eyes she had never forgotten, hard and grey, the grey of granite, of gunmetal, of a sunless sea in winter. He was mean and dangerous, and *still* scared her. She did not want him anywhere near her.

'Excuse me,' she said, 'but I'm rather puzzled as to exactly what I can tell you. I've only just arrived, and I don't even know you.'

And I'm becoming a brazen liar, she added to herself.

He shifted his weight slightly, raising one hand to lean against the frame of the patio doors, and Nicole observed unwillingly the ripple of muscle along his arm, the fine line of dark hairs from wrist to elbow.

'You will have to excuse *me*,' he said, but without a hint of apology in the words. 'I'm used to people knowing who I am. I'm Steve Rodriguez, and for starters you could tell me how you came to be driving through France with my daughter.'

The icy disapproval in his voice made it all too clear that he was not here to offer his thanks for the service.

'It's very simple, Mr Rodriguez,' she said. 'Sonia asked me to bring Lacey, since I was on my way here, anyhow. I had assumed she explained the arrangement when she phoned you.'

'Your assumption is incorrect. She phoned, true enough, but since I was not at home, she only spoke to my housekeeper, whom she informed that Lacey was on the way to Spain with a friend of hers. She then left the hotel without leaving any forwarding address, so I had no means of checking this information.'

His voice was still icily calm, but there was anger lurking just beneath the frozen surface. Nicole was beginning to feel angry, too, mostly with herself for not having realised that Sonia was a scheming bitch who had lied to her outright.

What a charming, well-matched pair they make, Nicole

thought grimly, and in retrospect she began to feel some sympathy for Lacey, who had been morose and disgruntled throughout the journey.

'I don't see the problem, Mr Rodriguez,' she shrugged. 'I presume you've seen Lucey, and she's all in one piece? Alive and kicking? Anyone would think I had kidnapped her, and was here for the ransom money.'

He studied her for a long, reflective moment, the strange, deep grey eyes looking into her and through her. He was sizing her up, as though she might indeed be a potential criminal, judging her and finding her suspect. Her hands were icy, and she clenched them to prevent them from shaking. Time, they said, was a great healer. It wasn't true. It was only a mighty amnesiac, which had allowed her to forget, until today, how much she hated this man.

'Be facetious, if it amuses you, Miss Nicole Bradbury. That's your name, I believe? I arrived home shortly after you deposited my daughter there, to learn that she'd travelled half-way across Europe with someone her mother bumped into in a bar.'

His lip curled disdainfully, and Nicole thought resentfully that it made her and Sonia sound like a couple of drunken harpies, instead of two lone women enjoying an aperitif.

'Look, Mr Rodriguez,' Nicole said determinedly, 'I object strongly to the implication that I might have done Lacey any harm. I ask you—do I *look* like a child murderer?'

The merest shadow of a smile touched his mouth, but it was scornful and derogatory, and she was not reassured by it.

'Now you come to mention it, no. You look like a student on a youth opportunities scheme,' he replied.

Nicole's face flushed angrily. She spent most of her office life disguising her slim figure in businesslike suits and pinning up her long hair, but for travelling she saw nothing wrong with jeans, sweatshirts and sneakers.

'It can be dangerous to judge by appearances,' she said hotly. 'And if you are not happy about Lacey's having travelled with me, you had better take it up with Sonia.'

'I intend to—just as soon as I find out where she is, which won't take me too long, now I know she was heading for Venice,' he said ominously. 'An hour on the phone should track her down. I know most of her watering-holes.'

And I wouldn't like to be her when you do catch up with her, Nicole thought.

'Fine,' she said briskly. 'Just so long as you sort it out between the two of you. As for me, I'll think twice before I do anyone any favours in future.'

A razor-edged tension born of anger and something less readily definable quivered in the air all around them. He regarded her again, but this time differently, seeing all of her, as a woman, measuring and evaluting what he saw.

Nicola had not known until this moment that being looked at by a man could be such a physical experience. So ruthlessly intimate was his gaze that she felt stripped and exposed. She shivered, hot and cold, insulted and embarrassed . . . and yet, when he lifted his eyes to her face once more, it was as though the warm and pleasurable caress of silk had been abruptly snatched from her.

And while she was still regrouping her stormed senses from this visual assault, he drew his wallet from the back pocket of his trousers and opened it up.

'Don't do *me* any favours, Miss Bradbury. I don't need them. How much are you out of pocket on my daughter's expenses?'

Nicole stifled an indignant gasp. He was the last person on earth—the very last—from whom she would accept money. He had taken everything her family had, once, but she had striven hard for her independence, and wasn't about to surrender any part of it to him.

'Nothing!' she said emphatically. 'I have no intention of accepting any money from you, Mr Rodriguez. Lacey's here, safe and sound, and let that be an end to it. Besides, Sonia gave her all she needed.'

Not strictly true. Lacey had run out of pocket money half-way through France, and she had an inordinate appetite for Cola-Cola and *pain au chocolat.* But she wasn't going to tell him that.

'She did?' He shrugged, and Nicole had no way of knowing whether he believed her, but he did not labour the point. 'Oh, well, if that's so, you could say I already paid. All part of Sonia's European grand tour, for which I'm footing the bill. Perhaps you have done me a favour by keeping her off my back. It's easier to write a cheque.'

He spoke lightly and without any discernible emotion, and Nicole's mind flashed back to Paris, and Sonia, knocking back the drinks and saying flippantly, 'He's loaded, is Steve. Absolutely loaded. And what do I get out of it? Half that filthy lucre should be mine, by rights. He cheated me out of it.'

Join the club, Nicole had thought wryly. But Sonia was shrugging off a Gianni Versace jacket as she spoke, and she'd booked herself on the Orient Express to Venice, so maybe she, at least, had had her pound of flesh. There had to be a pay off for being Steve Rodriguez' wife, and Sonia clearly wasn't anyone's doormat. Nicole could not be hypocritical enough to be sorry the marriage had failed. He had money and power, and that was what he had wanted above all. Personal happiness he did not deserve.

'If that's all, Mr Rodriguez, I really would like to get on with my unpacking,' she said distantly.

His shoulders rose and fell, opening up the splendid ribcage beneath the silk shirt, and what passed for a smile, the briefest glimmer of humour, enlivened the spare austerity of his features.

'Suit yourself, Miss Bradbury. But I don't advise you to unpack too much. It's hardly worth it for a stay as short as yours will be.'

Her chin went up instinctively as she recognised a threat, however veiled, and the adrenalin of apprehension pumped through her veins.

'With respect, Mr Rodriguez, that isn't for you to say—or to know. My reasons for being in Puerto de Castello are my own business. And don't you think it's rather unfair to attempt to browbeat me simply because you're angry with your wife?'

'*Ex*-wife,' he said, with quiet but heavy emphasis. 'And that has virtually nothing at all to do with it. You say it's not my business, but this is my home, and I *make* it my business to know what happens to it, and in it. And you . . . you'll correct me if I'm wrong . . . are here on behalf of a British tour operator known as Sunstyle.'

Nicole suppressed the gasp of incredulity which rose in her throat. She had been here less than an hour, and already he knew who she was, and what was her purpose. The implications of this filled her with a chill foreboding until, taking a firm grip on her reactions, she reasoned out for herelf how he had come by this knowledge. Lacey had told him.

'You aren't mistaken, but I still fail to see how it concerns you,' she said.

He glanced swiftly at the slim gold watch on his wrist. 'It concerns me greatly, but I don't have the leisure to go into detail right now,' he said, with cool formality. 'I might have an hour to spare later this evening. Shall we say eight o'clock at the Bar Nautico, on the quayside?'

He didn't trouble to wait for a reply, his confidence taking it for granted that she would have to be there if she wanted to find out what he meant. Only as he reached the door of the cottage did he turn back and say comfortingly, and with apparent seriousness, 'Don't worry—I shan't tell anyone.'

Nicole's throat was as parchment-dry as a waterless desert.

'Tell anyone what?' she demanded, striving to conceal a sudden rush of guilt.

'That you talk to yourself, of course. Yes, you do. I heard you when I came in. But your secret is safe with me.'

Relieved beyond belief to be alone again and free of his unnerving presence, Nicole realised that she was shaking, and although anger was primarily responsible, she could not deny that it was laced with a strong dose of fear.

Your secret is safe with me. He didn't know the half of it. He could not possibly have recognised her, and there was no way he could connect her with the man he had wrecked ten years earlier. That being so, it was uncanny that he should use those particular words.

He can't hurt me, she told herself firmly. She was here as the representative of a reputable and successful organisation, going about its legitimate business, and she could not see why he should object to that.

Nicole was tempted to ignore his command . . . it couldn't rightly be called an invitation . . . to meet him at the Bar Nautico.

But she was not so foolish as to succumb to this temptation. She, above anyone, was well aware that it would be lunacy to turn one's back on Esteban Rodriguez and hope he would go away. He wouldn't. Nothing he said was meant idly, and nothing he did was without a carefully thought out conclusion.

Glancing up from stacking a neat pile of lingerie in the drawers of her dressing-table, she caught sight of her reflection in the mirror above them. For a moment her pale face and wide, uncertain eyes reminded her too closely of the scared fourteen-year-old she had once been . . . *he* had once caused her to be.

'If I'm a fish on a hook, he's a bloody great piranha!' she said challengingly to the girl in the mirror, and forced a grin. 'So I talk to myself? There are worse vices, and I dare say Esteban Rodriguez is acquainted with most of them!'

Not staying long, was she? She'd see about that!

Even with the nerve-stringing prospect of a meeting with Steve Rodriguez at the end of it, walking around Puerto de Castello in the warmth of the evening was like meeting again an old and valued friend not seen in years, and finding that, miraculously, the friendship was as true and as affectionate as ever, and could be picked up where it had been left off.

She stood for a few minutes on the quay, where boxes of colourful fish were being unloaded from half a dozen large fishing-boats which had just put in, watching the instant drama of the auction. Smiling, she wandered on along the small promenade which hugged the waterfront, circled by shops and cafés, all doing brisk business in the warm evening hours which followed the long afternoon siesta. There was no shortage of people shopping, drinking, or simply standing around talking; in fact, the entire population of the village seemed to be out and about.

The sheer pleasure of being involved in and surrounded by this cheerful way of life reassured and uplifted her momentarily, diverting her from the serious purpose of her errand. So the shock hit her fierce and hard as she rounded the curve in the waterfront and came abruptly upon the Bar Nautico.

There were classier drinking places in the village, and subconsciously she must have expected Steve Rodriguez to have chosen one of them as his rendezvous. Maybe that, as much as the tricks the years played with memory, had caused her failure to make the mental connection when he suggested this one.

The Nautico was where the fisherman drank. It was dark and noisy inside, full of male laughter and a flickering television set which never seemed to be switched off, but there was an outside terrace beneath a striped awning, virtually on the beach, with boats drawn up alongside, and water lapping the sand only inches away.

She could see Teddy now, an aficionado of local bars, well into his second or third Fundador, puffing contentedly at a Havana, waiting for her to finish her own contented rambles round the village and join him for an ice-cold Coca-Cola. Usually she would be hungry, too, and unable to hold out until dinner, and he would say indulgently, 'Well, young lady, looks as if I shall have to buy you *tapas* again . . .'

Nicole gulped, overcome, and sank on to one of the cheap plastic chairs under the awning, fighting hard to get a stranglehold on her emotions.

'*Señorita?*' The waiter was at her elbow immediately, very young, polite and attentive. But Nicole was beyond speech right then, and could only gaze up at him dumbly, like an idiot. Why hadn't she remembered? Anywhere but here would have been preferable. She could not sit here and listen to Teddy's enemy tell her why he found her presence unwelcome.

'Having communication problems already, are we?' The long shadow falling across her, the soft, distinctive voice prepared her for the lean, savagely amused face of Steve Rodriguez. 'I'm surprised you can't get along in Spanish, Miss Bradbury. You'll need to. This is not yet one of those villages where tourists outnumber the locals, and all the bars are run by sunseeking expatriates.'

Nicole hardly heard the soft-spoken order he gave the waiter. Her senses were paralysed by the unpleasant innuendo in the quiet, but no doubt carefully chosen words.

What malign instinct had guided him to choose this place, out of a score of others, as if he knew that by doing so he could hurt and disorientate her?

Taking a deep breath, she responded as calmly as she was able, 'I *do* speak Spanish, Mr Rodriguez, adequately, if not brilliantly. The waiter simply caught me unawares. I was miles away.'

'Were you? That's odd. I would have said you were very much here,' he observed casually.

'It's just an expression,' she said with coldly laboured patience. 'It means that I was thinking of something else.'

He sat down, stretching out his long legs easily in front of him.

'I know what it means. I don't need lessons in a language I was speaking well before you were born,' he said. 'And if you'll heed my advice, never take up poker—not without a crash course on concealing the emotions that rather expressive face tends to reveal too easily. It was betraying thoughts of a painful nature a few moments ago. Just as, right now, it's making no secret of the fact that I'm not exactly your flavour of the month. Now why, I'm wondering, should that be so, when we scarcely know one another—do we?'

CHAPTER TWO

THE waiter brought two glasses of cognac and a tray of *tapas*, the appetising bits and pieces Spaniards were addicted to, and which all bars seemed to serve.

'I'm not hungry,' Nicole said icily. 'And I don't drink brandy.'

He shrugged with deep unconcern.

'You do, now. Don't worry about the *tapas*. He'll take away what we don't eat. As dinner is rarely eaten before ten in Spain, we've become a nation of inveterate snackers.'

Nicole was lying about her lack of hunger. The last time she had eaten was a skimpy lunch at the frontier with Lacey who, determined to hate everything Spanish, had complained loudly and insisted on hamburgers and French fries doused in tomato ketchup. She was ravenous. Her mouth watered and her gastric juices worked overtime on the delectable array of mussels, prawns, pieces of octopus in their own ink, bits of tripe and cooked rabbit, olives and all manner of salads. She stuck her hands in her lap and resisted firmly.

'Please yourself,' he said, biting an olive and taking a sip of cognac. 'I thought you might find it easier on a full stomach to explain precisely why you don't like me.'

'The onus isn't on me to explain anything,' she retorted. 'Are you so universally beloved that it comes as a shock when someone refuses to conform to type?'

The ghost of a smile, the merest hint of upturned corners softened that hard mouth, reminding Nicole that in the past he had always looked grim and implacable, and that was the way she had remembered him.

'No,' he conceded. 'There must be those who don't like me, but usually they have a reason. More often than not it's because I've beaten them to something they wanted.'

'Oh, well, if you want reasons, Mr Rodriguez, I can give you several. You haven't exactly behaved in a manner guaranteed to endear yourself to me, have you?' she said, speaking glibly, quickly, anxious to dispel the suggestion lingering in the air that she was predisposed to hate him. True as it was, he must not suspect it, or he would start wondering why, and he was altogether too sharp to let it stop at wondering.

'You burst in on me uninvited, and berated me for innocently giving your daughter a lift,' she continued. 'Then you threatened me about staying in Puerto de Castello. It's hardly the stuff on which great friendships are founded, is it?'

Disregarding the rest of her speech, he homed in on one word, eyes narrowed to granite slits, mouth once again unsmiling.

'I did not threaten you, Miss Bradbury. I simply stated a fact, if you will recall my exact words. You and your employers are wasting your time here. Nothing personal, I assure you.'

Without knowing what she was doing, Nicole reached out, picked up a mussel, and ate it. She was thinking very carefully, wondering what he had against Sunstyle's proposition, and not really aware that she was eating as she thought. But, once having tasted, it was difficult to stop.

'Irresistible, aren't they?' he said, clearly enjoying her surrender to temptation. 'Go ahead. He's brought more than enough for two, and I can't eat the lot myself.'

Nicole dropped a prawn back on to the plate as if it had bitten her.

'I don't know what Lacey has told you about my job with Sunstyle——' she began, but got not further, as he silenced her with a harsh, humourless laugh.

'Lacey, when I saw her for all of five minutes, was too busy plastering her room with Duran Duran posters to spare much time for conversation with me,' he stated baldly. 'I'm a businessman, Miss Bradbury, and I didn't get to be chairman of more companies than I'll bore you with listing by being uninformed. Sunstyle is investigating the possibility of taking over a property-letting agency, and you are here to do the reconnaissance work—correct?'

'And I see *you've* been doing your homework.' Nicole's voice was studiedly calm, but inwardly she was in a ferment. How could she have been naïve enough to convince herself she could come to this part of Catalonia and avoid this man? She should have been guided by her gut reaction of unwillingness when her boss, director Peter Delamere, had suggested that she would be the ideal person to look over the properties because of her understanding of Spanish and her prior knowledge of the area. And Peter's younger brother and co-director, Adrian, good-looking, flippant, and one to avoid in empty lifts and at office parties had flashed her a lecherous wink across the room, and agreed that she should go.

Absent-mindedly, her fingers strayed towards an olive. 'I wish you would tell me what you have against the idea of my company taking over this agency,' she said carefully.

'Willingly.' He drained his glass and signalled the waiter for another. 'Look around you, Miss Bradbury. What do you see? A village—a Spanish village by the sea—going about its everyday affairs. Fishing, vineyards, shops, and all the other normal, commercial necessities. A balanced mix of locals and people with summer villas, and, yes, a few discerning tourists who have made it here under their own steam. You've been here before.'

The inflexion didn't change on the last four words, to indicate that it was a question. It could equally well have been a simple statement of fact. Nicole swallowed hard—there was no sense in resorting to more subterfuge than was absolutely necessary.

'Yes—some years ago. That's one of the reasons Sunstyle sent me to do the assessment.'

He nodded briskly, completely businesslike and impersonal.

'Quite. So you will appreciate how little it has changed in those years, when parts of Spain which were once like this, are now unrecognisable. Puerto de Castello is not Brigadoon, Miss Bradbury. No one has cast a magic spell to keep it as it is. The reason you won't find amusement arcades and fish and chip shops is because those of us who call this home have fought hard to ensure that doesn't happen.'

'Oh, I get it,' she said, injecting a little mild sarcasm into her voice. 'You disapprove of tourists. Those who work hard all year round but don't enjoy the benefits of a benevolent climate, as you do, should not be allowed to share in all this for a short while, even if they pay for the privilege—or not on *your* doorstep, anyhow. No matter if it happens to bring prosperity and employment to the area ... that doesn't interest you too much, Mr Rodriguez, since *you* already have both!'

She had embarked on this verbal attack calmly enough, but somehow her own emotions of hatred and distrust had intruded into what she had intended as a hard but objective judgement. And now she was afire, not simply with righteous indignation on behalf of her future customers, but with a darker and more complex desire to hit out at Steve Rodriguez.

But it would not do. That was not what she was here for, and she should ... no, she absolutely *must* ... separate her own resentment, however justified, from the reasoned professional arguments her employers had a right to expect her to make.

Picking up the untouched brandy glass, Nicole drained the contents in one fierce, hopefully calming gulp, then looked up to see the unrevealing grey eyes of her opponent regarding her without any apparent disturbance.

'Feel better for that?' he asked levelly, not making clear whether he meant the hasty drink or the release of her scorn. 'I must say, for a woman who doesn't drink brandy, and wasn't hungry, you aren't doing too badly. Are you ready to stop being juvenile now, and join the adults?'

The fine skin of her forehead just below the hairline began to prickle, heralding a telltale and unwelcome flush of chastened anger, because there was just enough truth in the accusation to make it difficult for her to deny.

'That's offensive,' she said.

'And it wasn't offensive to brand me as a latter-day Luddite who resents progress and only cares for his own comforts? If you dish it out, you have to be able to take it, you know,' he pointed out. 'Of course, it goes without saying that I appreciate that tourism is big business in Spain, and necessary for the economy. Far be it from me to knock any legitimate way of making money. But over-commercialisation can ruin the very aspects of a place which make it attractive, and I won't have this village and its surroundings destroyed by mass tourism.'

'But Mr Rodriguez—if you'll forgive my saying so, you're barking up the wrong tree.' She smiled, and couldn't resist a slight dig at him . . . a small enough indulgence compared to the dressing-down he had just given her. 'Another expression I assume I don't have to translate for you. Sunstyle has no intention of altering the essential character of Puerto de Castello. We don't cater to that kind of tourist. Our customers are individuals who do their own thing, at their own pace, usually with their own transport. They'll love this place as it is . . . as I do, and as you do yourself.'

There was a short silence. Nicole studied her companion's face covertly but thoroughly, and found it gave no quarter. The lips were tight and unyielding, causing the grooves either side of them to deepen visibly, and there was no suggestion of compromise in the pewter-hard eyes.

'You're young and idealistic.' He shrugged cynically. 'I won't insult you by doubting your innocence and the honesty of your intentions. But if you had moved in the world of business for as long as I have, you would know how easily a corporate image can alter—with the nature of its board members, for instance. A different hand on the helm . . . a change of policy . . . a takeover by a bigger, brasher concern. In the face of any of these eventualities, could you guarantee what you are telling me now?'

Again, the shadow-smile, mildly derisive.

'Of course you couldn't,' he answered his own question without giving her the opportunity to speak. 'Before you know it, we'd have high-rise hotels, coachloads chartered in from Gerona airport, and the place swarming with hordes of screaming singles whose idea of a good time is to drink themselves into near-oblivion and leap into bed with whoever is available.'

Nicole jerked out of her chair, burning with outrage at this misrepresentation of her purpose, but he was on his feet almost as quickly, instantly destroying any advantage she had hoped to give herself, perfectly relaxed, yet poised for any action which might be required.

The tension mounted unbearably. Nicole felt that if she did not break away, something inside her would snap like an elastic band stretched too tightly. But she was trapped firmly by the intangible force of his will, like a mesmerised rabbit in the glare of a car's headlamps. Instinct told her that if she moved he would not hesitate to enforce that same will physically, and the thought of being touched by him sent tremors of shivering ice down her back.

'Anyone who tries to introduce that kind of scenario here

. . . no, I'll go further than that . . . anyone who takes the first step along the road that might lead to it, I'll fight, and, make no mistake, I'll win,' he warned softly, his voice devoid of anger, devoid of all passion, but conveying none the less a firm and all too credible intent. 'I usually win, because I have this rooted aversion to losing, and I shan't be too fussy about what weapons I use. So show some sense, take yourself off home, and tell your masters it's not on. All right?'

He held her in that invisible spotlight for a few seconds longer, and then, abruptly, she was released and set adrift. There was only the jingle of coins he had tossed on to the table to pay for the drinks, and the lithe figure threading its way through the strolling groups, raising an airy hand in greeting now and then until he finally disappeared from view.

Only the fact that he had accused her of being juvenile prevented her from beating her fists on the table-top in an excess of frustrated fury. Who the hell did he think he was, laying down the law to her as if this were his own private kingdom, and he alone made the rules which governed it? Catalonia had been rich in mediaeval warlords once, but this was the twentieth century, and surely no one man could wield that much power? He might have finished off Teddy, but she had come up fighting, and was not about to have him dictate what she could and could not do.

Sunstyle would have that agency if it killed her, if only to prove to him . . . and to herself . . . that, just occasionally, Steve Rodriguez could lose. The more bitter he found defeat, the sweeter would be her triumph, and in that white-hot moment, there was nothing in Nicole's life that matterd to her quite so profoundly.

Because she was young, healthy, and tired after a long day on the road, Nicole dropped asleep as soon as her head hit the pillow on the narrow bed of dark, reproduction Spanish oak. But she was woken very early by a strange throbbing sound which increased steadily, resonating through the still air, and although she could not identify it, somewhere in the recesses of her mind a memory stirred.

So compelling was this half-forgotten echo that she slipped out of bed and tiptoed up on to the roof terrace. It was that breathless moment when the world hovers on the edge of morning, the air cool and faintly resinous, birds beginning to twitter desultorily, and a blue translucence lightening the sky. Across the silent rooftops she saw a dozen fishing-boats putting out from the harbour, lamps ablaze, and realised it was the sound of their engines which had disturbed her. She sighed, moved and reassured by this traditional symbol of Mediterranean life which the hectic progress of this frenetic century had not eroded.

Her gaze lifted to the wooded hills, where Vistamar lay hidden. You could watch the fleet setting out from the vantage point of its balconies or simply lie peacefully in bed, listening to the engines thrumming. Was *he* awake and listening, or still asleep, refreshing himself for yet another day of steam-rollering anyone who stood in his path?

You're in danger of becoming obsessed by that man, just as Teddy and your mother were, she told herself sharply. In the last years of his life, moping out his enforced retirement in a soulless bungalow on the outer reaches of Worthing, Teddy had found a morbid fascination in watching the rise of the Rodriguez star.

'Don't torment yourself, darling,' his wife would reply soothingly. 'We still have each other, and Nicky—and that detestable man will get what he deserves one day, I know it!'

Teddy would not hear of Nicole's leaving school and getting a job to help out financially. He insisted she took up her place at university, and somehow, she never knew how he managed it, there was always a cheque at the beginning of every month, to supplement her meagre grant. Although —and she smiled with wry affection at the memory—by mid-month he would often be on the phone, hinting that things were a bit grim, the heating bills had gone up, the rates were in, and if she could let him have fifty pounds he'd straighten it out next month, of course . . .

'Teddy, you don't *have* to send me money,' she had insisted, stepping up her protests when Lorraine began to suffer from a debilitating and progressive illness. 'I *can* manage, truly. Lots of students have to.'

'Nonsense!' he'd said, and the cheques kept coming, and she kept on refunding the cash to him. And he must have salvaged something for, after his death, his solicitors assured her that there was sufficient to pay the bills for the nursing home where her mother's last months were now being rendered as peaceful and painless as was humanly possible.

A shadow of grief flitted across the girl's face as she gazed out over the rooftops, seeing not the silken, azure sea and the apricot dawn rising over it, but her mother's drawn face as she rested against her pillows in the bright, sunny room at St Anthony's Hospice.

'You mustn't think of giving up your job, Nicole, after you've worked so hard to get where you are. Dear Teddy would be so proud of you, and so am I. Besides, what more could you do for me if you were here?'

It was true. The skilled, compassionate care involved in nursing the terminally ill which Lorraine received at St Anthony's was the best she could have had anywhere. Sister Cornelia had told Nicole, with kind but unsentimental practicality, 'If you stop work to be near her, your mother will panic and think the end is closer than it really is. Let her go in good time, with peace and dignity, happily thinking of you making your way in the world. Keep on sending your lovely letters and pictures, and we'll get in touch with you through your office if we need to.'

Nicole had to see the sense behind this reasoning, but she knew she would worry about her mother while she was away. Lorraine's condition had definitely deteriorated since last summer when, although Nicole had been busy on the French camp sites as always, she was only a short drive and ferry-hop away from home. But her mother was for the most part free of pain, and oddly enough, seemed content and passive. Only when she spoke of Steve Rodriguez did her eyes come alive, and blaze with the passion of hatred in her pale face.

By now, Nicole knew that if she went back to bed, sleep would evade her. Slipping into a skirt and T-shirt, she let herself out of the house and walked slowly through the still quiet village, along the promenade to where the beach petered out into the rocky shoreline.

Lorraine, she knew, blamed Steve Rodriguez for every misfortune that had overtaken her, up to and including this final tragedy, but now, gazing down into the translucent turquoise water, the thought troubled and nagged at her—could it be right or fair to make one man accountable for so much?

She sighed, resenting the confusion which had begun to plague her, disturbing the normal clarity of her thought processes. It wasn't consistent to be cursing him one moment and falling over herself to be fair to him the next. Better . . . well, easier, at any rate . . . simply to carry on singlemindedly detesting him, and allowing no creeping doubts. After all, he had not been fair to *them*.

Seated on a rock, she slipped her feet out of her shoes and dangled them in the water which still held the chill of night. It was so clear that she could inspect the varied species of marine life without difficulty . . . that intriguing plant, for instance, with the colourful leaves, just beyond her reach . . .

The shock as she slipped off her perch gave her a jolt, and for a moment she expected to land fully clothed in the water, but bracing her foot on a half-submerged rock, she recovered her balance just in time. But as she did so, something sharp stabbed the fleshy pad just beneath her big toe, and she exclaimed aloud in pain. Scrambling back to the beach, she examined her foot, relieved to find no sign of a cut or gash, nothing bleeding, and no apparent damage.

Nicole put her sandals back on and set off back to the village, but by the time she reached the quay she was limping, the agony shooting through her foot each time she put it to the ground. She had definitely done something to it, and knew she was not going to make it all the way to the cottage without the relief of a short rest. Sinking down on to a wooden bench on the quayside, she removed the sandal again with a groan.

A number of small fishing-boats had returned from a night's work fishing the inshore waters, and boxes of shining silver sardines were being unloaded, but the men politely took no notice of the lone English girl, and went about their own business, laughing and shouting to one another.

Briefly diverted from her own problem, Nicole watched as another boat put-putted in across the bay. There were two men aboard, and as they leapt out to pull their craft in across the shingle, she frowned, aware that there was something familiar about one of them. It wasn't simply that he was less deeply weatherbeaten than his companion. The instinctive symmetry of his movements, the turn of his neck and the ripple of muscle along his shoulders, identified Steve Rodriguez at once. There was an inimitable quality about him which ensured that he would stand out anywhere.

But on a fishing-boat, wearing heavy denims and a sweatshirt, a thick navy sweater knotted loosely by the sleeves around his neck? For a moment she forgot the throbbing pain in her foot, and stared, astonished. And because she was an unexpected and discordant element in the early morning scene, he spotted her immediately, his forehead creasing in displeasure.

She wished he would simply ignore her, as the others had, but knew there was very little hope of that wish being granted. He spoke briefly to his companions before striding across the quay to look down at her, arms folded, mouth unsmiling.

'Don't you think this is a little voyeuristic? It's barely seven o'clock, and these men have been working all night. They aren't a spectacle for visitors to goggle at.'

'Good morning to you, too,' she said pointedly. The combination of the pain, increasing every minute, and the stinging disapproval of his attitude did not put her in a benevolent mood, and she thought it appropriate to remind him of his own lack of courtesy. 'I wasn't aware I need your written permission to take an early morning stroll. Nor was I "goggling" at anyone, until I recognised *you*. I was surprised to discover that you were a part-time fisherman.'

If, in her annoyed response to his manner, she had injected an element of derision into her words, it went badly off-target. He wasn't in the least offended by the description.

'It's as good a way as any I know of counteracting the tensions of business,' he said easily. 'Yes, I know one could have a yacht, or a speedboat, but there isn't the concentrated discipline of knowing a catch must be brought in—or the camaraderie that goes with it.'

And that was probably what had surprised her most of all—the sight of this powerful commercial magnate, perfectly at home among the rough and ready fraternity of the quayside.

'They're friends of yours?' she asked curiously, and was rewarded by that half-smile she had already begun to know so well.

'I used to come here in summer when I was a small boy. If my father could not get away, my mother would bring us, my sister and myself. Victoriano and I used to fish together with a line from the end of the jetty. Now he lets me go out in his boat occasionally. He knows I'll earn my passage. I'd make a tolerable fisherman, if all else failed!'

If all else failed. But it wouldn't. Reduced to the ownership of one boat, in a year or so this man would be operating a fleet. Nicole pushed away the image of a brown-legged boy runing wild with the children of the village, a boy who belonged to a family . . . father, mother, sister . . . it did not tally with her idea of the man she somehow imagined had sprung like a fully fledged demon into their lives ten years ago.

His attention moved from her puzzled face to the bared foot.

'What have you done to yourself?'

'Oh . . . nothing much,' she said hastily. 'I trod on something sharp in the water back there.'

'Among the rocks? Let me see.'

'No . . . I told you, it's nothing.' Why was she always doing something slightly foolish whenever he appeared? Talking to herself, sitting dumbstruck at café tables, stumbling into the sea.

'I said let me look.' His voice cut through her protests sharply, and he squatted on his haunches in front of her. Closer to him than she had yet been, she became aware of odd flecks of silver in the dark hair at his temples, and the deep grooves either side of his mouth looked as if they had been ingrained there by harsh experience. It was a face that had lived hard and with concentrated purpose, sparing its owner no more then *he* spared others, co-existing with a taut, athletic body expected to take as much punishment as he demanded without questioning its reserves of stamina and energy. Together they emitted potent but entirely unforced vibrations of quietly confident masculinity, a steady but powerful signal it was impossible to ignore.

He took her foot in hands both capable and more gentle than she had expected them to be.

'You've trodden on a sea-urchin and part of a spine has lodged itself in your toe,' he said. 'Don't you know to wear plastic shoes in the water near rocks? I thought you were a seasoned traveller.'

Only now she remembered belatedly the plastic sandals they had bought each year from the shop which sold gear for the beach.

'I hadn't intended to be in the water,' she pointed out. 'And it's some years since I was by the Mediterranean. Usually I spend the summers on one of our camping sites in the Vendée. The coastline there is sandy, not rocky like this.'

He shrugged. 'They say we learn by our mistakes. However, this will have to come out. A sea-urchin is a living creature, and that thing will work its way deeper into your flesh until you end up with an infected foot and a painful session in the hospital out-patients' department. It should be removed while it is still relatively near the surface. Can you walk, do you think?'

She nodded. 'I think so. I'd better go home.'

'Come along then. I'll get it out for you. I'm an old hand at this,' he said briskly.

Nicole stood up more quickly than she had intended, and a shaft of red-hot agony pierced her sole, so that she almost collapsed again.

'It's all right! I'll manage!' she gasped. The thought of being confined within four walls with him again induced in her such a blind, irrational panic that she would gladly have limped to the nearest hospital step by painful step to prevent it.

'Don't be foolish,' he said dismissively. 'Unless you're a contortionist, this is one job you can't do half so well for yourself.'

He hooked an arm firmly round her waist to relieve her of the necessity of putting her weight on the injured foot. His fingers bit into the sensitive space just below her ribs, and she felt the heat from them spreading upwards along her diaphragm and the valley between her breasts like a shooting golden fountain of warmth.

The mere thought of his touch had made her shudder with fear, but now, in the space of a few minutes, he had touched her twice, and Nicole was deeply astounded to discover that her own body was not shrinking from him with repugnance. Instead she knew a strange, nervous exhilaration, a surge of the life-force, as if she had pushed the accelerator of a powerful car to the floor, and felt the engine stride forward in response.

'I have the feeling you're none too comfortable,' he said, a note of wry amusement creeping into his voice. 'Try putting your arm around my neck, and see if you can hobble.'

Too right I'm uncomfortable, Nicole thought frantically, as her tentative hand slid along his shoulder, feeling the shift of musculature beneath the sweatshirt, and then the hard, dry warmth of his neck, with the dark hair just curling over the tips of her fingers.

He turned his head to look down at her, and for the first time she saw a full, genuine smile deepen the creases either side of his mouth, transforming his face as a burst of sunlight through thunderclouds brightens a stormy sky.

'The trouble is you're not tall enough to use me effectively as a crutch,' he murmured, a wicked, lively humour sparkling in his eyes. 'Why suffer unnecessarily?

I have a better idea.'

He swept her legs from the floor, crooking an arm under them while the other cradled her shoulders. More than the ground was snatched from beneath Nicole. Could a man feel this warm, this clean, this good, could he smile that way and still be an unscrupulous, double-dealing cheat?

She had once played Ophelia in her university drama club's production of *Hamlet*, and some lines ran wildly through her head as she was carried through the streets feeling foolish and flustered and perplexed, aware only peripherally of the soft laughter of the fisherman and the tolerant smiles of old women opening their front doors—all no more than a background to the living, breathing warmth of Steve's chest, the steady, forceful drum of his heart, hopefully drowning the agitated flutter of hers.

> 'Oh, villain, villain, smiling, damned villain!
> . . . meet it is I set it down
> That one may smile, and smile, and be a villain;
> At least I'm sure it may be so in Denmark.'

At least, it certainly is in Spain, she misquoted inanely to herself as they reached the door of the cottage.

CHAPTER THREE

STEVE lowered Nicole on to the cane sofa in her living-room.

'With you in a minute,' he said, and disappeared into the kitchen as though this were a house he had lived in all his life. She heard sounds—running water, drawers being opened—and he returned in a short while with antiseptic cream, tweezers and sticking plaster. 'A good thing you brought a first-aid kit along.' He knelt at her side.

Once again he was far too close for her to feel at ease, and she fixed her gaze on a point on the wall opposite, as he set about his self-appointed task. She gritted her teeth, determined not to whinge.

He was remarkably adroit and speedy. She felt him probe with the tip of the tweezers for the fine, miniuscule point of the spine, then there was one swift moment of agony as he grasped the thing and deftly withdrew it.

But although she was silent, he must have noted the stiffening of her body.

'It's done. You can relax now,' he said, dabbing the reddened area with antiseptic cream and covering it with plaster. 'It should be all right now, but if you have any trouble you must get proper medical attention.'

She had to look at him then, since their eyes were on a level, she seated on the sofa, he still half squatting, half kneeling at her side, and she became acutely conscious of particular aspects of him . . . the brown wrists below the sleeves of the sweatshirt, the blue growth of stubble along his jaw—he *had* been up all night, and needed a shave—the tensed muscles of his thighs keeping him perfectly balanced

35

in what a less finely tuned body might have found an uncomfortable position. Nicole ran her tongue round the inside of her mouth in an attempt to banish an exceptional dryness.

'I took the essential step of putting on the percolator first, so there should be coffee soon,' he said.

My God, had he even noticed *that?* she wondered. Did he also know that it wasn't thirst that was causing this parched sensation, but an unreasonable nervous excitement? She desperately hoped not.

'I must say, you were remarkably stoical,' he observed. 'I'm sure it was extremely painful, but you didn't make so much as a murmur.' This disconcerting praise was not given without a sting in its tail, a note of faint sarcasm creeping in as he added, 'Ten out of ten for the old Dunkirk spirit—dogged determination in the face of adversity. A national characteristic, isn't it?'

'Why ask me? You should know the answer to that yourself,' she retorted spiritedly. Realising belatedly that she might have made a gaffe, she added quickly, 'Lacey told me your mother was English.' Nicole saw the merest flicker of emotion animate his eyes before the poker-face closed up again.

'She was—although Lacey scarcely knew her, or my father. They died when she was just a baby.' He volunteered no more information, although obviously it could not have been a natural death from old age. 'But don't be deceived by my family tree. I'm a Spaniard—and more particularly, a Catalan.'

She shrugged, affecting a faint it's-all-the-same-to-me kind of smile.

'Should I need to know that?'

'Yes. The word was rapped out swiftly. 'Put it this way—you'd be a fool to disregard it. To use a bulfighting metaphor—this is my *querencia.*'

Nicole raised deliberately bored eyebrows.

'Bullfighting is all Greek—or should I say, Catalan—to me, Mr Rodriguez,' she informed him.

'Then let me enlighten you.' The deceptive quietness of his voice raised the follicles of hair on the nape of her neck. 'The *querencia* is the spot in the ring to which, for some reason not apparent, the bull will keep returning, because there he feels at home, feels safest and strongest. On this ground it is unwise to challenge him, because he is likely to be at his most dangerous.'

She laughed. 'Right. I'd have to be pretty thick not to work that one out, wouldn't I?'

'Wouldn't you?' he agreed softly. 'And I don't think you're thick, although I have a feeling you may be a mite stubborn, Nicole.'

She thought—this is not real. They were talking about bullfighting, but that wasn't really what it was all about. He was leading up to something else, and she didn't trust him in this pleasantly devious mood any more than she had yesterday, when he was direct and rude.

The room was still and quiet, full of a hazy sunlight floating through the patio windows, and the scent of fresh coffee beginning to drift in from the kitchen, accompanied by the soft burble of the percolator. Nicole did not move, pinned to the seat by the persistent gaze which was no longer harsh, but penetrating and speculative. Like a laser, it seemed to burn away the shielding layers of deception behind which she hid her real self, so that they were no more protection than were her thin summer clothes against his slowly savoured appreciation of her body. She could not have felt more defenceless.

What was incredible, but beyond denial, was that there was something insidiously seductive about that very helplessness . . . a treacherous weakness that insisted she could do nothing about this, and was in no way responsible for anything that might happen to her as a result. The signals from her brain to her body were jammed by a sexual current of powerful intensity, blotting out thought, reason and sense—a frightening but intoxicating removal of her will.

He was leaning forward slightly, and she knew he was going to kiss her. Knew also that she wanted him to. Right now, it had ceased to matter if she feared and distrusted him. What mattered was to know what it felt like to have that hard, remorseless mouth on hers, and only then, with the abrasive reality of physical contact, would she have the full measure of this tormenting enemy. Her chin tilted upwards of its own volition, her face was drawn towards his, as she went willingly to meet the inevitable.

But the kiss never came, and she was unprepared for the lean, casual fingers that negligently hooked themselves beneath the strap of her camisole T-shirt and slid it down her left shoulder, baring it to the swell of her breast

She drew in her breath, because she was all too obviously bra-less beneath the brief garment, vulnerable to the questing finger that traced its way along the pale curve beneath the faint beginnings of her tan, unhurriedly pushing the material before it. The tender skin of her breast prickled and she felt it stiffen with anticipation as his hand moved inexorably downwards.

Nicole did not know how it happened, but somehow she became separated from herself, watching from afar, observing as well as experiencing the delicious, sinful and unholy eagerness with which she waited for his touch, and reaction swept over her, in a douse of self-disgust as cold as iced water. Whatever motivated this man, it was not passion. She could not discern an atom of real desire for her in his expression. The name of the game was not pleasure, but domination.

'Mr Rodriguez—Steve,' she said, with a trace of languid amusement in her voice, 'has anyone ever told you that you lack finesse? Can you honestly expect to turn a girl on with such a decided pong of fish?'

There was a moment's lapse before his reaction came, and even that was unexpected. He threw back his head and laughed—genuine, open-throated laughter, the first she ever remembered hearing from him, either now or in the past.

'You don't find fish aphrodisiacal?' he chuckled softly. 'Victoriano swears his wife does—which is just as well, I imagine!' With clinical exactitude, he hitched the strap back on to her shoulder, heaving an exaggerated sigh of mock regret. 'Never mind—I have an appointment at the bank in Figueras at ten o'clock, so I couldn't have spared you the dedicated attention your charms undoubtedly merit.'

Nicole shivered with shameful anger. She was almost certain that he had had no real intention of making love to her. It was poker again—he had been bluffing, sure that her nerve would break.

'The bank will open on a Saturday morning especially for you, will it?' she asked disbelievingly, letting him know she had seen through his subterfuge.

'It will today. This is an extraordinary meeting of the board, and I'm the chairman. It's the only time this week I had free.' He stood up, stretching easily. 'I had better call in at my apartment in Figueras and shower off the Essence of Fishing-Boat. If I'm going to ask a member for his resignation, the least I can do is put on a clean suit and a tie.'

Nicole knew a creeping, scalp-prickling sensation of *déjà vu*. Someone was going to get it in the neck this morning, just as Teddy once had, all those years ago. Did he know? Were he and his family waiting with dread for the axe to fall?

'Why is he going to be fired?' she asked, almost in a whisper, driven by a horrified curiosity and an irrational fellow-feeling for this total stranger.

He looked at her hard, the teasing amusement all gone, the steeliness back in his eyes, chasing out the humour.

'Incompetence.' The word dropped like a stone into the silence between them. 'There is only one thing I am less prepared to tolerate, and that's chicanery.'

Nicole turned her head away abruptly, almost choking on the bitter ire in her throat. How could he say it—he, of all people? Had he forgotten how he forced Teddy Walton out of business? Or was there one law for the sharks who had risen to the top of the pond, and another for the hapless creatures who had to inhabit the same waters? Minutes ago, she, too, had suffered a lapse of memory, and had forgotten herself sufficiently to tremble under the touch of his hand. Now she only wanted to be rid of the sight and sound, and the feel of him.

'Well, don't let me detain you from your work,' she said, laying a slight, unpleasant emphasis on the last word.

'No one detains me unless I've a mind to let them,' he replied easily. 'Look after that foot, won't you, and steer clear of all the local hazards—marine or otherwise.'

After he had gone, she drank two cups of scalding hot coffee without tasting either. Less than twenty-four hours had passed since he came back into her life, but there wasn't one of those hours she hadn't had him on her mind, and she was alarmed by her own behaviour this morning. Nicole knew men—she'd studied alongside them, worked with them, dated them—but only superficially. She had needed desperately to work hard and get on, to attain a measure of independence and success which couldn't easily be taken from her, so she had had no time for deep relationships and no inclination for swift affairs. She was a total stranger to the perverse but eager desire she had known when Steve touched her.

She saw only one way out of this labyrinth, and that was through work. She must survey all the properties on her list without delay, write her report, and get back to head office as quickly as possible.

Oh, yes? Even to her own ears it sounded like a vast over-simplification. What if Sunstyle went ahead, and Peter decided to send her back here to manage the agency? Was she to refuse, and what plausible reason could she give for turning down a plum promotion which they both knew would be a milestone in her career? Yet if she did come back, Steve would still be here. Would there not at some time have to be a reckoning?

Three frustrating days later, Nicole was beginning to wonder if she would ever be in a position to have to make this difficult choice. She had spent those days walking around the village, driving up into the hills around it, looking at the properties and talking to the owners, trying to convince them of the benefits of having an organisation like Sunstyle behind them.

She had not expected it to be difficult. For a number of years the letting had been done by a small, moribund firm who had left it more or less to its own devices. Bookings had never increased and in some instances were on the decline. Nicole met the owners—some of whom were local people, others lived in Figueras or Gerona—and explained to them that with good management and publicity in England, and the services of a rep on the spot, they could double their profits.

She met with unfailing, smiling politeness everywhere, nods, handshakes, cups of coffee, glasses of wine from the local vineyards, gifts of fruit and of fish caught the same morning, endless good wishes for her health and happiness—and endless evasions and procrastinations. Not one owner agreed outright that he would sign the new contract, although there was a lot of *'quizas'*—maybe—and much shrugging of shoulders.

Why? It was so obviously a good deal and in their own best interests, there had to be more behind their reluctance than natural caution and conservatism. Some of the owners were vintners and landowners, still deep in their peasant roots, but others were businessmen from the towns, who understood clearly what they stood to gain. But still they resisted and would not commit themselves.

Nicole did not have to search her mind very deeply for the cause of this reluctance, and she did not think she was being paranoid in suspecting the hand of Steve Rodriguez. *You're wasting your time . . . there's nothing here for you or your employers . . .* in some way, he had to be putting pressure on them, and she wondered darkly if they were the victims of a kind of subtle intimidation. There were always such means, if you had power. Possibly his bank held mortgages on their property, or they were otherwise in debt to him, or, as a major employer in the area, members of their families depended on him?

She began tentatively to insert his name into the conversation, fishing delicately for any hint—a word, a frown, anything, although she did not expect anyone to come right out and commit financial suicide by admitting they were being pressurised to stall her.

But . . . it was odd . . . the reaction was quite the reverse to the one she sought to confirm her fears. Mention of Señor Rodriguez produced only smiles and praise and universal respect. More than that, she could not deceive herself, she was left with an impression that he was not only admired as a real *'hombre'*, a local boy who had made good, but was liked personally, as a man. She came across several instances of help and kindness on his part—someone's vineyard had gone through a bad patch, but Senor Rodriguez had arranged an interest-free loan to tide it over, someone else's son wanted to study in America—Senor Rodriguez had fixed it up with his old college, and paid the boy's fare. Señor Rodriguez had obtained a specialist for someone's mother suffering from a rare blood disease . . . and so it went on.

Could it be gratitude, she wondered in astonishment, rather than fear, which had made these people fall in with his wishes? If so, that was an insidious but equally unpleasant form of coercion. After all, their livelihoods were involved, and to make them pay for past help in such a manner was about as low as anyone could go.

He's capable of it, Nicole thought glumly, toying with a cup of coffee on the terrace of the Bar Nautico. She had hoped to have her survey finished and her report written by the end of the week, but at this rate, it wasn't going to make encouraging reading for Peter and Adrian. The area was ideal for the kind of client they hoped to attract, the properties were delightfully situated, but she had failed to persuade the owners to renew their contracts with Sunstyle when the old ones ran out.

'Hi.' Distracted from her gloomy thoughts, Nicole looked up to see Lacey standing by her table. It was the first time she had seen the girl since depositing her at Vistamar, and she wondered anew, not without sympathy, how two such handsome people as Steve—even *she* could not deny his attractiveness—and the gorgeous Sonia had managed to produce this lumpy girl.

It had to be said that Lacey did not help herself. If she would stand up straight instead of slouching and hunching her shoulders, the improvement in posture would make her appear slimmer, and no one could look pretty wearing a permanently dissatisfied expression. On the plus side, she had a good skin and lovely eyes, and in a year or two, if she fined down, a real stunner of a swan might emerge from behind these unpromising duckling feathers.

Nicole put her own problems aside and summoned up a smile. She had not acquired a particular fondness for Steve's daughter on the journey down. Most of the time her manner had been sullen and uncooperative, verging on insolence. But she was young enough to remember how it felt to be fourteen, and plain in one's own eyes, and how demeaning it was when adults simply looked through you as if you were of no consequence.

'Hello, Lacey. How's it going? Have you settled in all right?'

The girl slumped despondently on to a chair.

'I guess so. I'm about as welcome as a pork chop at a kosher wedding, but I knew all along my father didn't want me here, so that's no big deal. He never has wanted me, so why should he start now?'

Nicole was on the horns of a dilemma. There was rarely smoke without fire, and if Lacey felt unwanted, who was she to say glibly, 'I'm sure that's not true'? And why should she fall over herself to do or say the right thing by Steve Rodriguez, who probably wouldn't recognise a moral scruple if it ran up and bit him on the leg? On the other hand, she could not help recalling his unfeigned anger that first day, when his daughter had turned up in the care of a stranger. He had acted like . . . well, like a father.

'Oh, I don't know,' she said cautiously. 'Parents aren't always easy to read. He was pretty mad about my giving you a lift when I hardly knew you. Tore a strip off me, good and proper.'

Lacey managed a feeble smile. 'I'm his property, aren't I? He doesn't allow anyone to mess around with anything that's his,' she said. 'The only thing he's ever interested in where I'm concerned is school—how I'm doing at school, what college I'll go to, what subjects I want to major in.

He's red-hot on higher education for women. You'd think he'd invented the idea.'

Well, bully for him, Nicole thought sourly. It irked her that anyone so detestable as he should champion such a thoroughly laudable cause.

She was therefore surprised to hear herself saying, 'It *is* important, Lacey. Your future depends on it,' and thought, oh hell, I'm taking *his* side again.

'No, it doesn't,' Lacey contradicted rebelliously. 'See these old women, out in the vineyards? They probably left school at twelve, got married at fifteen, and had half a dozen kids in as many years, but they look happy enough to me. I reckon I'd be better off finding the right guy, sticking with him, and having a *proper* family.'

The envy in her voice made Nicole ache.

'There's nothing wrong with that ambition, in itself,' she agreed. 'But a bit of education and a few years under your belt might help you recognise the right guy when he comes along.'

'It sure didn't help my folks much,' Lacey said smartly. 'They got married when they were at college together, and look what happened to them. That's another thing about my father. *He* pleased himself whom he married, and made a real mess of it, but now my Aunt Juana has this boyfriend he doesn't approve of, he's doing his best to split them up. I don't think it's any of his business. She's probably older than you.'

This last comment caused Nicole's eyebrows to rise in mild amusement.

'All but past it,' she said gently, signalling the waiter and ordering a Coke for the girl who was perspiring freely in the heat. 'Does your aunt live with you at Vistamar?'

'Only at weekends. She runs a chain of fashion boutiques in Gerona. Owned by my father, of course, so he has her over a barrel, doesn't he?'

Something nagged at the back of Nicole's mind and then vanished again, like a tune she was trying to remember, and couldn't quite. She turned her straying attention back to Lacey.

'That's a useful kind of aunt to have.'

'Humph! Not for me. None of her clothes fits anyone over a size ten,' she snorted resentfully. 'They're all designed for midgets. It's all right for you—you'd look a dream in cropped trousers and baggy shirts. I'd just look like Miss Piggy!'

It was hard work trying to say anything that hit the right note, but Nicole persevered doggedly.

'We all change. At your age I was as skinny as a beanpole, and convinced I'd never fill out in the right places. If you take after your mother, you'll have a lovely figure.'

Wrong again. But at least she had succeeded in amusing Lacey, who hooted with malicious laughter.

'Oh, yeah! She's for ever giving up this or that to keep it, especially when she has a new boyfriend, and that's fairly often. She lived on yoghurt and lemon juice for three weeks before we came to Europe!'

Sonia, the perfect, streamlined size twelve, with everything stacked just right, had to diet to stay that way? You never could tell, Nicole thought, although she certainly hadn't noticed Steve's ex stinting herself on the gin and tonics.

'There's a . . . boyfriend at the moment, is there?' she surmised.

'Oh, sure. Why do you think Mom was so keen to unload me on you? She's meeting him in Venice. Well, she could have just stuck me on the plane, else, and let my father meet me this end, like she did last time I came, two years back. I mean, the stewardesses look after you, and you can't get off the wrong stop, can you?'

Nicole was inexpressibly saddened by the girl's offhanded

acceptance of her mother's peripatetic sex-life. In spite of his success, she reflected, Steve had failed to give his daughter a stable upbringing. Divorced parents, continents apart, a mother who swapped lovers as frequently as diets, and a father who found her an inconvenience at best did not constitute an ideal background for a teenage girl.

This should have afforded her a grim satisfaction, a kind of meagre triumph, and would have, only days ago, but oddly, it didn't, now. All she felt was a lingering, sorrowful regret for so many messed up lives—Teddy's and Lorraine's, Sonia's, Lacey's . . . and, to a certain extent, her own . . . all on account of one man's overweening ambition. She wondered if his conscience ever troubled him, or if he considered so much human debris to have been a price worth exacting.

After Lacey had left her and wandered off morosely along the beach, Nicole abandoned the now cold remains of her coffee and followed her nose in the direction of the shop which sold spit-roasted chicken portions. One of these, together with a bag of *fritas,* would solve the problem of her lunch, and instead of going back to the cottage, she could pick up her car from the square and drive straight off to view two villas a little way along the coast.

She was actually waiting in the queue for the chicken when it hit her, so blindingly obvious that she cursed her own stupidity in not having seen it before.

'He had her over a barrel,' Lacey had said, with youthful cynicism. Of course—*of course.* No wonder he could afford to be so smugly confident that she, Nicole, would not succeed in her purpose. If she refused to back off, if she sent in a favourable report to her directors, all he had to do to prevent Sunstyle taking over was to buy the agency himself. He was probably going ahead with the negotiations even now, and that was why she had met with so many negative reactions.

'Now why didn't I think of that?' Nicole said aloud, to the puzzlement of the man roasting the chickens. One thing was for sure, now that she had: she must move—and fast.

CHAPTER FOUR

AN HOUR later she was in her car on the way to Figueras, having made an urgent phone call to head office and been lucky enough to catch Peter working through his lunch break.

'We've got competition,' she told him tersely. 'A local big shot, name of Rodriguez, who also happens to be an international business tycoon. Have you heard anything about this at your end?'

'Not a whisper.' Peter sounded doubtful. 'I've heard the name, of course, but not in connection with our bid. Are you sure of your facts—I mean, is there evidence to support what you say?'

'Not exactly,' Nicole admitted reluctantly. 'It's more of a gut feeling I have, after talking to the property owners. They're holding back, and I'm convinced *he's* behind it. Peter, I know my report isn't in yet, but it will be wholly favourable. The area's perfect—still unspoiled, yet with enough to do and see all around, and the properties are basically sound. Can't you up your offer a bit and clinch the deal quickly, on the strength of that?'

'And be left with an agency and a load of owners who won't let? Nicole, we can't move into the area without local goodwill.'

'I could try again,' she persisted. 'I know the contract is fair as it stands, but with perhaps a little more inducement . . .? It's a winner, Peter, I know it is, and we can't stand back and let it be snatched from under our noses!'

'Hold on a minute! Your enthusiasm is commendable, but I get the feeling there's more to it than meets the eye,'

Peter observed shrewdly. 'So far, all we have to go on are your suspicions. You'll have to give me more than that. Then we'll see.'

'All right. I will,' she vowed forcefully, annoyed that he couldn't, or wouldn't, see what was so clear to her. She put the phone down, and moved from one room to another until finally she came to a stop in front of the mirror in her bedroom.

I'm not fussy what weapons I use.

Maybe *she* had weapons, too. She surveyed herself critically, and, taking out the grips, shook her hair loose over her shoulders, smiling seductively at her reflection. What she really needed, in order to find proof of her suspicions, was some time alone in Steve's office, and she could not afford to stake out the building and wait around until he conveniently vacated it. A workaholic such as he could not be relied upon to down tools and head for home at five p.m., either. He needed bait.

So? He was a man, wasn't he—no doubt as to that. Beneath that cold surface she divined a raw sexual energy as strong as all the others he possessed. He was available, and surely as susceptible to temptation as any other man. She had never taken on the role of seductress before, but desperate times demanded desperate measures, and anyhow, she had no intention of following through and delivering what she promised.

The drive to Figueras took her over the shoulder of the mountains by way of a tortuous road between great, barren, lion-coloured hills . . . an austere, unyielding land which reminded her ominously of the formidable opponent she was on her way to deceive.

The tower blocks of Figueras, the largest commercial centre in the area, were visible long before she reached it and fought her way through the traffic-choked streets towards the address she had looked up before leaving.

She had expected Steve's headquarters to be one of the tower blocks, but, surprisingly, it was a Gothic-style Victorian building not far from the central *plaza*, which would have looked at home in Threadneedle Street. Nicole avoided the official company car park and found one a few blocks away, from where she walked the short distance back.

Imposing oak and glass doors led her into a spacious, marble-floored hall with a huge, curving oak desk manned by three receptionists. Nicole approached the youngest and most sympathetic-looking of these, a redhead with upswept hair and a friendly smile, and in her best, most precise Spanish, she said, 'Good morning. I should like to see Señor Rodriguez.'

'You have an appointment?'

'I'm afraid not.' Nicole smiled back apologetically. The receptionist's manner remained friendly, but she shook her head with discouraging firmness.

'Without an appointment, that will not be possible. Maybe there is someone else within the organisation who can help you? What company do you represent?'

Her tone implied doubt that Nicole was sufficiently important to merit an interview with the man at the top. Brushing her hair back languidly, she glanced down at the desk, murmuring softly, 'I don't. It's personal.'

She could feel the receptionist looking her over, summing her up, and it was obvious what conclusion she reached. Nicole did not blame her. She had dressed the part, in a sleek, black, fitted dress she had bought for a party last summer. It was sleeveless and fastened from the deep V-neck to the hem with tiny jet buttons, the bottom three of which she had left undone, so that an enticing expanse of slim leg showed as she moved. Her hair was brushed out so that it swirled around her face, emphasising the blue wideness of her eyes, and the lips moistly glossed with pink, and a cloud of Madame Rochas perfumed the air as she turned her head.

'Señor Rodriguez does not see anyone on personal matters during working hours,' the red-haired girl said primly.

'Oh, I know that—and I wouldn't normally dream of disturbing him,' Nicole agreed, with effusive approval. 'I'm sure you're absolutely correct to abide by that rule, but this is very important, and will only take a matter of minutes. I don't think he would be very pleased if he wasn't told I was here,' she added, still smiling, but dropping just the hint of a threat.

She intercepted the glance that sped between the receptionist and one of her collagues and knew that she was not the first to have attempted to run this gauntlet.

'I'll have a word with his secretary,' the receptionist conceded, neatly passing the buck. 'I doubt she will be able to help you, but perhaps she will take a message for you.'

'Thank you so much,' Nicole said sweetly, her voice dripping with gratitude. 'Tell her that my name is Nicole Bradbury.'

She watched with carefully concealed nervousness as the other girl rang the extension, and a brief conversation ensued, which she was not allowed to hear. If Steve refused to see her, the entire plan flew out of the window. She held her breath and prayed that his curiosity would be strong enough for him to make an exception to his own rule.

Evidently it was. The redhead turned towards her, and with an air of faint surprise, said, 'Señor Rodriguez says he can give you five minutes. His secretary is on her way down.'

The secretary was smart rather than beautiful, thirtyish, and married, Nicole noted, catching a glimpse of her hand. They rode up to the fourth and top floor in an iron-grilled monstrosity of a lift which looked almost as venerable as the building, and not a word was spoken throughout.

They emerged into an atmosphere of hush almost worthy of a cathedral. The reception area and the other floors she had glimpsed as the lift passed them were busy with people going about their tasks, but up here there was an air of rarefied dignity. The plain but obviously high-quality carpet on the floor of the corridor they trod, the dark oak doors with solid brass handles, the lofty proportions and high ceilings designed in a more expansive age, were all more reminiscent of a select club than the hub of a business empire. But the secretary's office with its filing cabinets, word processor and VDU screen were familiar territory to Nicole. She allowed her eyes to do a deceptively languid reconnaissance of where everything was as she waited to be ushered into the sanctum sanctorum.

The secretary buzzed her employer respectfully on the intercom, and then said, still a shade disapprovingly, 'Señor Rodriguez will see you now, Señorita Bradbury.'

Steve's office was right at the end of the corridor, the intervening two doors being shut, so she had no chance to see what lay behind them. She heard him say, 'Thank you, Señora Roig,' and then the door closed behind her, and she was alone in the lion's den.

'Nicole,' he said evenly. 'This is a singular pleasure. I ought to make it clear that I don't allow staff to entertain personal visitors, so as a rule, I abide by that dictum myself. If you wish to see me on business, it's usual to make an appointment first.'

He spoke dispassionately, and while he did not betray any trace of the pleasure he mentioned, his censure was milder than she had expected. Contradictorily, this put her on her guard, far more than she would have been if he had blasted her out.

Automatically, her eyes had flown to the desk on entering, but he was not seated behind it. He was standing over by the window, cool and immaculate in a summer-weight suit of pale grey, which made his eyes appear dark by comparison. Behind him, Venetian blinds filtered the bright Spanish afternoon sun to a bearable level, essential since, this being the corner suite, the windows occupied almost the whole of two walls.

Nicole glanced quickly around, not merely from curiosity, but acting on an instinct which told her that there were clues to any man in his surroundings. She was not sure how she had imagined his office to be, but knew her imagination had not conjured up this. The desk and cabinets were not oak, as might have been expected, but smooth black ash, the carpet a pale champagne, there were squashy beige leather chairs, a large, healthy bay tree in a tub, and on the walls a number of works of modern art.

'Well, Nicole,' he said finally, and she felt his slow, inch-by-inch appraisal of the tightly fitting black dress clinging to the curves of her body. 'I take it you are here for a purpose, and I'm a busy man.'

Nicole did not need the lessons of her drama club days to inject a frisson of nervousness into her voice as she crossed the room, her swift, fluid steps revealing a flash of leg with each soft movement of her hips.

'I realise that, and I'm sorry to burst in on you like this,' she said breathily, biting her lip a little, and looking down at the carpet, then up into his face again, her blue eyes full of a wondering apprehension. 'But I *had* to see you. I couldn't stop thinking about the other day, and, well . . . how rude I was to you.'

'Ah. You mean I didn't really smell fishy?' he said, with straight-faced seriousness. 'Shame on you, Nicole. It wasn't true, and there I was, thoroughly cast down and mortified.'

It did not take too much acumen to deduce that he was quietly laughing at her. Nicole knew she might have expected that, but all the same, it was difficult to suppress her natural inclination to turn her back and walk out. But having got this far, she could not give up so easily.

'Make fun of me if it amuses you, but I'm trying to apologise, and to thank you properly for taking that wretched sea urchin out of my foot. I don't usually forget my manners,' she told him.

'Oh, I believe you. What I don't quite believe is that having remembered them, you felt obliged to drive all the way here in your best bib and tucker, and cajole your way into my office,' he said. '*Very* touching, but I'm sorry, Nicole, I just don't buy it. Why don't you come right out from behind the smokescreen and tell me what it is you're after?'

Nicole would have been seriously disappointed in him if he had believed that her sole purpose was in observing the rules of courtesy. A phone call would have sufficed for that, which he knew as well as she did. But her satisfaction in leading him on was marred by a sick excitement in her stomach. It was impossible to view him objectively, as prey, feeling like this. He was close enough for her to observe minutely the rise and fall of his chest beneath the shadow-striped silk shirt, and the waves of natural warmth emanating from his body made her oddly faint. Her nostrils breathed in a suggestion of aftershave spiced with sandalwood. She could almost feel the texture of his skin beneath her hands, almost taste his mouth on hers, and the lines between pretence and truth wavered and became so blurred that she could no longer keep them in sight.

Without warning he moved, and she found herself backed into a secluded triangle between the wall and the leafy bay tree in its tub. Nicole knew that this was all going dangerously awry. She was no longer in control of the plan she had conceived, or at all sure she could pursue it any further. Her best hope was to drop the whole thing and get out, but his hands were on her shoulders now, their sinewy strength forestalling any sudden attempt to cut and run.

'You're looking very different today, Nicole—very alluring and sexy, one might say. I'm receiving a very different signal from the ones you usually send me.' Again she was subjected to that sensual scrutiny which was almost as erotic as his touch. 'Is this all for my benefit—the cleavage, the legs . . . not forgetting the overdose of perfume? How flattering. You should be more careful. I could be excused for getting the idea that you fancy me, and we both know where that might lead.'

Nicole turned her head to one side, trying to avoid both the taunting eyes and the teasing voice. But there was no escape. His hand turned her face firmly towards him once more, then stroked the underside of her chin as he tipped her head back. Brushing beneath her hair, he twisted it into the thick strands just above the nape of her neck, with a little tug which was painful yet tantalising. Her head fell back slightly, pushing against the pressure of his hand, and she began to tremble like a blown leaf, waiting with barely concealed anticipation for him to kiss her, and knowing that she had been waiting ever since that moment at the cottage.

'You're not fooling, are you?' he asked with faint surprise.

All the clever little words of enticement she had planned to say to him in order to lay her bait, deserted her in the face of this intense physical compulsion. She gave him the bitter truth, because she was no longer in any state to pretend.

'No . . . and don't think I like it, because I don't . . . but I've never felt like this before,' she blurted out with painful honesty.

Very lightly, teasingly, his mouth touched the corners of hers, giving her just a little and no more. He was playing with her, testing the strength of her need, and, as she was sickeningly sure it was intended to, this taunting approach only aroused her more fiercely. He brushed her lips lightly, making her wait, and those few seconds of unbearable anticipation were the longest she lived, until at last, firmly and unequivocally, he gave her what she was silently pleading for.

His kiss took the air from her lungs, leaving her empty and breathless. She was invaded and conquered, drained of resistance and left with no place to retreat. His mouth moved from hers only to nip gently at her earlobe, and from there roamed pleasurably along her throat, his hand all the while twined in her hair, keeping her head fixed and immobile, at his mercy.

'Steve!' she gasped, pushing her hands against his chest in an instinctive gesture of protest, as she felt the change in him from light amusement to the determined strength of aroused male desire. 'Please . . . the window . . . anyone could see us!'

'Nicole——' He raised his head, and his eyes probed her face, bewildered, panic-stricken, but still naked with wanting. 'We're on the fourth floor, and not overlooked. And this isn't the day for the window-cleaners. But if it worries you . . .'

He reached out and tweaked the cord of the Venetian blind, plunging the room into a striped and shadowy twilight. Patiently, but without any intention of being thwarted, he removed the barrier of her hands, letting her arms fall limply to her side, and began unfastening the jet buttons down the front of her dress, slowly and carefully, one after another.

'You're wearing your bra today—how disappointing,' he murmured. 'Still, it isn't much of an impediment.' His hands pushed aside the thin lace of the cups to enclose her breasts, and she gasped with the exquisite agony of pleasure so fierce and sweet it was only a shade away from pain.

'Oh, don't . . . please . . .' she half choked, knowing even as she said them that the words were only half meant. 'What if someone comes in . . . your secretary . . .'

'I don't know what kind of secretaries you employ in your office, but mine would never dream of bursting in without buzzing first,' he assured her, unperturbed. 'Relax, Nicole. You know you're enjoying this. Isn't it what you came for?'

Was it? In some awful, Freudian sense, was this what she had wanted all along, her real purpose only a blind flung up to hide it? Nicole no longer knew.

The telephone shrilled out obscenely, loud and insistent in the hot silence of the room. It jolted them back out of the deep, primal absorption of a man and woman lost to everything but each other. For one taut, splintered second, Nicole thought he was going to ignore its summons, then he straightened, shrugged, and let her go, the tension running out of her with the release of his hands.

'Duty calls,' he said philosophically. 'Don't go away.'

She leaned against the wall, needing its solid support, her breath coming quickly as she half listened to him talking quietly but with deadly firmness about exclusion clauses on a contract to build a shopping centre in a town the name of which she knew she would never remember. Never had the aphorism 'saved by the bell' rung quite so true. Shakily, she ran nerveless hands through her dishevelled hair. She was aware that he had stopped talking and replaced the receiver, but she still gave a little, nervous start when he reappeared, soft-footed, at her side.

'Cold feet, huh?' he said lazily. 'What a pity—it was just beginning to get interesting.'

Maybe—just maybe—Nicole thought, as reason began to reassert itself, it was not too late to salvage something of her scheme, after all.

'It's not a question of cold feet,' she contradicted huskily. 'You just don't pick the right time . . . or the right place, Steve.'

He pulled open the blinds, allowing sunlight to flood into the room, and regarded her with a steady, questioning gaze.

'So? If this is an invitation you're issuing, perhaps you'd better tell me the time and place,' he suggested. 'The ball's in your court, Nicole.'

She took a deep breath, deliberately, like a swimmer about to plunge into a pool of unknown depth.

'What time will you finish work?' she demanded boldly.

Dark eyebrows rose in carefully modulated astonishment.

'You mean today? What did I do to get this lucky?' he asked, and she hoped he would attribute the sudden lowering of her gaze to a rush of shame at her own importunate eagerness. 'My last appointment today is at four-thirty according to Señora Roig. I usually stay on and catch up with some paperwork, but . . .' he let the sentence trail off, suggestively.

'But you needn't,' Nicole supplied. 'I shall be at my place in Puerto de Castello.'

He laughed, low in his throat, and with another of those swift movements which always took her unawares, caught her under the elbows with both hands, drawing her towards him. 'You like to make a man sweat for what he's about to receive,' he complained mildly. 'I have to drive all that way, when we could be at my apartment in Gerona in ten minutes from leaving here?'

She did not trust herself any closer to him, recalling just how easily he had demolished her resistance earlier, but somehow she could not prevent herself from sliding her hands up the lapels of his jacket.

'No—I mean, I've never been to your apartment, and I

would feel strange there,' she protested. 'You make me
nervous enough as it is.'

'If I make you that nervous, perhaps you should ask
yourself if you are doing the right thing,' he said levelly. 'I
don't much care for making love to a woman who doesn't
want it at least as much as I do.'

'But I do!' she said urgently, without thinking, seeing
only her hard-won triumph slipping from her grasp.

He took her hands in his, detaching them from his suit,
lifted them to his mouth and grazed the knuckles against the
edge of his teeth.

'Lady, it's not done to sound so eager,' he told her, his
voice low and sensuous. 'Don't you know you're supposed
to affect a little indifference?'

Nicole did not pull away from him. He did not know it,
but this was the last moment she had in which to savour this
novel and bewildering pleasure, the intoxication of being
close to a man—one particular man and no other. She was
back on course now, but even so, recalling the drowning
bliss of his mouth on hers, and the whisper-soft touch of his
hands, she was able to say with utter conviction, 'I know.
But would you believe me if I did?'

He let her go, reluctantly she thought, but did not answer
her directly. Then the intercom buzzed on his desk, and
Nicole did not linger. By the time she had reached his office
door and glanced back, he was already seated in the beige
leather executive chair, giving instructions to his secretary and scanning some papers in front of him at the same
time.

She closed the door resolutely behind her. Wishing would
solve nothing and, having come this far, there could be no
turning back.

In a large department store she bought a plain navy skirt
and a white blouse, the kind of outfit girls everywhere wore
to the office, and in the cloakroom she changed into it,

pinning up her hair into a prim top-knot and toning down her make-up. She grinned as she surveyed her handiwork. The siren had vanished and in her place was a working girl, neat and unobtrusive. Returning to where she had parked the car, she bundled the black dress into the boot, and set off back towards the Rodriguez office block once more.

It was four forty-five as Nicole walked across the marble-floored foyer. A number of people were about, passing to and fro, but she walked briskly, as if she had a definite errand, carrying in her arms a sheaf of papers which was actually a folded up newspaper. No one took the least notice of her, as she had gambled they would not. In a building this size, no one could possibly know everyone else who worked here.

It took a little surreptitious searching, but she found what she was looking for without too much difficulty—the ladies' room on the third floor. Locking herself into one of the cubicles, Nicole sat down to wait it out on the only seat available, listening to the rapid chatter of girls as they refreshed their lipstick and combed their hair at the end of the working day.

She waited quietly and almost motionless, her breath held, her heart thudding, and heard the familiar sounds of people departing, doors shutting, lifts clanging, and then the gradual fall of silence. With a shudder of distaste, she knew she was alone in the building, and must remain so until it opened for business tomorrow morning, when she would have to make an unnoticed exit, walking out as calmly as she had walked in.

The prospect of spending the night in a deserted office block was not alluring and, now that she had embarked on it, she began to wonder if the whole idea were not completely crazy. The night hours stretched interminably ahead, once the long May evening had closed in, and she knew it would be a give-away to switch on a light when the place was supposed to be empty. The time would pass with unwelcome, dragging slowness.

But if she could get a look at the files, and find anything at all which bore out her contention that Steve was planning to buy the agency himself, her ordeal would be worth while. Surely Peter would pull out all the stops if he knew the competition genuinely existed, and for Nicole, the world had narrowed dangerously down to a desperate battle to upstage Steve, to come out on top and make him taste a little of the bitter medicine of defeat. As she waited, the thought that this afternoon she had been almost ready to hand him another sort of victory only sharpened her need to triumph, now.

She remained in her hiding-place for the best part of an hour, cramped and apprehensive, before at last she heard the heavy-booted tread of men's feet passing along the corridor and up the stairs to the fourth floor. An age seemed to pass before they returned—she heard them check the lift before continuing on their way down to the lower floors. Then all was quiet again, but she made herself be patient, letting another half-hour elapse before she finally emerged from her hiding-place.

Her amusement faded, and she shivered slightly as she crept softly along the corridor and up the stairs. A deathly quiet pervaded the empty building, and yet it seemed to breathe around her, watchful and accusing. For the first time, guilt assailed her as she reached the carpeted sanctuary of the fourth floor, and she felt like a criminal. This was furtive and underhand, and had anyone told her, days ago, that she would conceal herself unauthorised in a building with a view to grubbing around in someone's private files and purloining information, she would have laughed outright in their face.

It simply was not her scene. Honesty, hard work and

her own talents had got her where she was, and so far, they had sufficed. Devoted as she was to her job, she had never envisaged herself descending to dubious and shady activities in her performance of it, and she knew with deadly certainty that, had the potential rival been anyone other than Steve Rodriguez, she would not be here now, with her heart in her mouth, and her emotions at cross purposes with her brain.

But here she was and, short of raising a hue and cry and giving herself up, she was here until morning. With renewed determination, Nicole pressed on. His office was locked, as she had fully expected it to be. But his secretary's was open, and with a sudden thrill of approaching victory she slipped inside, closing the door quietly behind her.

Where to start? A phalanx of filing cabinets, neatly indexed, holding files on all the Rodriguez companies and associated holdings, banking and financial interests, stocks, foreign subsidiaries. She had the whole night ahead of her, but she did not want to linger here longer than necessary. The security patrol would probably come round again, and she had no idea at what intervals it operated.

Her eyes flew to the VDU screen and she smiled with satisfaction. Of course—all data would be recorded and stored on computer, and it would be an easy matter to find out where the information she was seeking was located. Maybe she would not even need to search the files at all. Nicole sat down at the console, and switched on.

The moment her fingers tapped the keys, an unholy shrieking sound, like a police klaxon, split the air and resounded through the stillness. Cold with horror, she hit the keys desperately, searching wildly for a formula to turn it off. Frantically, she switched the terminal off, but it was no use—she had already activated the alarm and it kept on ringing, incessantly, the noise almost deafening her. Nicole jumped to her feet, and for a moment stood there, shaking with fear and indecision, her hands instinctively covering her ears.

She was galvanised into action, coming to her senses swiftly, with only one thought in her mind. She had to get out of here, away from this incriminating clangor she had set off. She had to find somewhere to hide, before she was discovered red-handed.

It was already too late. Booted feet were running down the corridor, and Nicole jerked open the door to come face to face with two burly, dark-uniformed security guards and a bristling Alsatian, straining impatiently at a short lead. She had blown it.

Nicole spent the next half-hour perched miserably on Señora Roig's typing chair, to which she was grateful in that it obliged her to keep her back stiff and unbowed, and she forced her chin not to let the side down by drooping wretchedly.

She had toyed with a wild notion of bluffing it out, pretending to have been working late and inadvertently to have pressed the wrong key, setting off the alarm. But it was useless, she realised. The guards knew she was not an employee, and that the building had ostensibly been empty when they patrolled it. So when they demanded her name, she gave it, and nothing more—no excuses or fabrications or pleas as to her fate. Name, rank and serial number, she thought grimly, wondering if the Geneva Convention meant anything to the man who occupied the managerial suite.

She was not questioned further. While one man stood over her, barely controlling the quiveringly eager guard dog, the other made a swift telephone call, and Nicole was unsure relief was an appropriate emotion when she strained her ears hard enough to deduce that he was not calling the police. From his quietly deferential tone, and the frequent murmurs of, Si, Señor Rodriguez,' she was left in no doubt as to who was on the other end of the line. Watching him set down the phone, she experienced a sinking of the heart. Once again she was at the mercy of Steve Rodriguez, and this time she could see no possibility of redemption.

She waited. No one spoke. The guards were silently impassive, and the dog growled softly in his throat once or twice, a warning Nicole did not need. The soft hum of the traffic in the street below carried easily in the quiet, reminding her of other people's lives going ordinarily and pleasantly on their courses, while hers had been reduced to a devastated shambles by her own crass ineptitude.

She heard the ominous clanking of the lift, then the lighter, but decisive, tread along the corridor, and felt dry-mouthed and light-headed, faint with the longing for this ordeal to end which she imagined victims might feel before a firing squad.

The door opened, and he stood framed in the aperture, deadly calm, hateful, his face as empty of emotion as if it had been cast in bronze. There was neither pity nor amusement in the grey eyes, now. They were as hard as black ice, and utterly unyielding. She faced him like a trapped fly in a spider's web, unable to move, certain of nothing but an unpleasant end.

With one spare gesture of his hand he dismissed the security men, and then slowly and menacingly he advanced on her, step by threatening step.

Nicole had nothing on her side. To the world beyond this room she was a wrongdoer, caught in the act. To herself she was no more than a fool on a fool's errand, too blindly impulsive to have let caution warn her that what she intended could never be that simple. And to the man closing in on her now, thumbs hooked arrogantly in his trouser pockets, wearing the expression of a Grand

Inquisitor facing a cut and dried heretic, she was a prisoner
without appeal, his to reprieve or sentence as he chose.
Drawing the tattered scraps of her dignity around her, she
uncoiled herself from the chair and got to her feet,
straightening herself forcibly. Whatever was coming to her,
she would take it standing, head up. That was the only
option left to her.

CHAPTER FIVE

IT WAS a long time before he spoke. Or so it seemed to Nicole as she waited, guilty and helpless, for him to take some action. Anything would have been preferable to this awful suspense—even if he had struck her, for then, attack being the best method of defence, she would have had some accusation to fling at him in return. But he did not allow her that. He was icily controlled and damnably correct.

'I expect you realise what a complete and utter fool you've made of yourself,' he observed at last, and the contempt in his voice made her cringe inwardly, although she continued to stand erect, facing him definantly.

In the face of her taut-lipped silence, he continued witheringly.

'Did you really think I fell for that sudden excess of passion routine you gave me this afternoon? "I've never felt like this before, Steve," ' he mimicked savagely. 'I have to admit, you were very convincing, for a while. I thoroughly despise a woman who demeans herself by using her body in such a manner.'

She found her tongue finally, if only because she could not bear to stand there and suffer this verbal lashing without putting up some resistance.

'You seemed more than willing to play along with it, all the same,' she retorted sharply.

'Why not, indeed?' He subjected her to a long, raking stare which reminded her deliberately of those uninhibited moments of abandon. 'A woman who behaves like a tramp shouldn't be surprised if she's treated like one. But it didn't really fool me, Nicole. If it had, I would have been on my way to Puerto de Castello, not sitting in my apartment in Figueras, positive that you were up to *something*.'

He paused, moved a step nearer to her, and it cost her a mint of courage to refrain from backing away.

'It didn't ring true, because I'd lay any odds you're still a virgin,' he said brutally. 'Reserved, well brought-up girls who have kept themselves untouched don't suddenly kick over the traces and offer themselves to a man quite so blatantly, even if they've fallen madly in love with him. Nice try, Nicole, but I've been around too long to be taken in by it.'

Nicole swallowed hard. There was nothing she could say to demolish this argument, because it rested on a solid bedrock of truth. He wasn't going to believe, now, that she had wanted him so badly she had not known how to handle it.

Her chin came up. Even if he were inclined to believe her, why should she give him the satisfaction of knowing he had that much power over her? She was sufficiently at his mercy as it was.

'Clever, aren't you?' she said stingingly. 'I suppose it offends your male pride to discover that a woman isn't exactly panting for you. All right, yes, I'm a virgin. I'm not ashamed to admit it. It isn't a crime, even these days, and I certainly had no plans to let you alter my status.'

He gave a derisive snort.

'You needn't worry. I wouldn't lay a finger on you, now. Contrary to popular English folklore, all Spaniards are *not* sex-obsessed Don Juans, but if I wanted to make love to a woman, there are enough around to ensure I don't feel deprived.'

'I'm sure there are, but, interesting as your amorous adventures must be, I'd rather you spared me the details,' she snapped back.

'Gladly. It's probably high time you were enlightened——' he paused meaningfully on the word '—but someone else can have that pleasure. All this is irrelevant, really. *You* are the one who is going to give details of what you hoped to accomplish here, tonight.' As she struggled to find words, he said sharply and impatiently, 'I'm waiting, Nicole. You can either talk now, to me, or you can tell your story to the police.'

'If you're going to hand me over to them anyhow, then I might as well take my chances with the police.' She shrugged, with a bravado she was far from feeling.

'Don't push your luck. Normally, my security people would have called them in straight away, before they even dreamed of troubling *me*,' he told her curtly.

This broke through her display of indifference, and her eyes flooded with bewilderment as she met his, wishing she could discern some recognisable human emotion there.

'You mean—you're only here because it's me? This is some kind of . . . preferential treatment? Thanks very much!' she burst out.

'Sarcasm isn't going to help you,' he pointed out calmly. 'I'm here because your name went to the top of my blacklist after our little . . . er . . . encounter, shall we call it? . . . this afternoon. Although I never imagined you would attempt anything *this* crazy, that you would assume my security was so lax you could get away with it! So talk, Nicole—for your own sake.'

She was swept by a frightening lassitude, an immense weariness which was a reaction to the suspense of the last hour.

'All right,' she said with a sigh. 'I had reason to believe you were planning to take over the agency, and I was looking for some evidence to support my suspicions.'

He stared at her so long and hard, she felt he was taking

her apart to uncover any shred of untruth in her words.

'Is that *all*?' he demanded incredulously. 'You went through all that . . . masquerade . . . exposed yourself to so much risk, took so much trouble . . . all for so very little?'

The implied disdain awoke a flicker of tired anger in Nicole.

'It might not seem very much to you,' she flashed back at him. 'But how else was I to find out?'

'Very easily.' He leaned back against the desk-top, hands resting on its flat, shiny surface, hips relaxed, legs stretched out, and although his expression and his manner were still gravely cold, some of the tension had eased out of him. 'You could have asked me, and I would have told you it was not so. Or is that too simple, too straightforward for you?'

A harsh laugh was torn from her.

'Oh, yes? And you would have told me the truth?' she challenged bitterly. 'You would have expected me to take your word for that?'

'You're in rather a precarious position to accuse anyone else of underhand dealings,' he reminded her. 'Let me see—you haven't damaged anything, so far as I can tell, and you didn't break into the building. On the other hand, you're on private property, unauthorised, and were caught seeking access to confidential information. Trespass, industrial espionage . . . one could almost describe what you were doing as theft. And since you were caught in the act by two unimpeachable witnesses, there would be little point in your pleading not guilty. Of course . . .' he hesitated fractionally to let her absorb the full impact of what he was saying '. . . a good Spanish solicitor might help. An English one wouldn't be well up on the finer points of Spanish law. Would Sunstyle foot the bill, do you reckon?'

'I wouldn't know,' she said through gritted teeth, all too aware that he was deliberately punishing her with this agony of uncertainty.

'No, of course you wouldn't. I should imagine it would be a new experience for a reputable organisation,' he said. 'Oh, Nicole—you *have* blotted their copybook, haven't you? What am I going to do with you?'

He was mocking her now, without a doubt, and Nicole could bear this nerve-tingling suspense no longer.

'Why don't *you* tell *me?*' she demanded. 'Since you are so obviously determined on turning me over to the law, you might as well get on with it.'

'Ah, but I haven't decided,' he said, surprisingly. And while she was still reeling from astonishment and relief, he straightened up and looked around his office, almost distastefully. 'Come on. Let's get out of here.'

He did not take her arm or propel her towards the door. He simply stood back and allowed her to precede him, without any indication that she might do anything other than comply. And indeed, Nicole was sensible enough to recognise that she had very little choice.

In the lift he kept a punctilious distance from her, and their shoulders did not even brush as they crossed the foyer together. *I wouldn't lay a finger on you now,* she remembered, and wondered why those words sounded so bleak.

She did not catch the quiet words he said to the guards, moving a little aside so she was out of earshot. But one of them sprang to open the doors, and Nicole emerged into the warm, sweet air of the Spanish evening, incredibly battle-scarred and years older in experience than the impulsive girl who had walked boldly into the building only hours earlier. Free—and yet not free.

'Don't imagine you are about to get off scot-free,' he said, reading her mind. 'I shall expect reparations of one sort or another, even if I don't take recourse to law.'

She glanced sharply sidelong at him, wondering just

what kind of reparations he would see fit to exact, and, catching her eye, he smiled grimly.

'I wasn't suggesting payment in kind, so there's no need to look so scared,' he said. 'I think I made it clear I'm not interested in any woman's body on those terms.'

'What makes you think I would offer it?' Even in as slippery a situation as this, Nicole could not bite back the retort.

'Maybe you wouldn't—not if you thought there was a chance you would have to deliver the goods,' he said cuttingly. 'But I thought I would spare you the embarrassment. Mutual and equal desire is the only real basis for such a relationship.'

Still without touching her, he steered her into the company car park like a helpless ewe at the whim of an alert and masterful sheepdog.

'My car's not here. I left it in a car park a few blocks away,' she said hopefully.

'But mine is,' he remarked, and so it was, a sleek white Mercedes sports with a black sun-top. He unlocked the door at the passenger side. 'Get in.'

'But . . . where are we going?' Nicole had panicky visions of the police station. Perhaps there was to be no clemency for her, after all.

'Get in,' he repeated authoritatively. 'You didn't think I was going to let you simply drive off into the sunset, did you?'

Nicole slipped quickly into the passenger seat. What was the use of protesting, when he held all the cards? Whatever he had in mind, however unpleasant it was, she had no defence but endurance. Somewhere, some time, this awfulness must come to an end and he must let her go.

He drove out of Figueras by the same route as she had come in, but by now she had learned it was wiser to keep her mouth shut and ask no questions about her destination.

Pinpricks of light had begun to pick out the city behind them, and ahead a great, golden full moon climbed theatrically over the darkening rim of the mountains. The silence of the hills was all around them, cool and mysterious, giving out a resinous scent as the heat faded. He switched on the headlamps, illuminating the twisting road as it hairpinned round the steep, sheer bends, doubly hazardous in the failing light.

Miles from anywhere they came upon a restaurant set back a little from the road, white and gleaming among the dark green of cork and pine surrounding it. Nicole had passed it on the way to Figueras, but now, although the lamps glowed softly inside, the car park was empty as he turned the car into it.

She looked at him questioningly, incomprehension written all over her face.

'It's a restaurant, Nicole,' he said, with exaggerated patience. 'Food—yes? I'm hungry.'

'I couldn't eat a thing,' she stated flatly, and he gave a derisive shrug as he switched off the engine.

'I seem to have heard that one before. Still, no matter. If you really don't want to eat, you'll have to sit and watch me, because I do.'

The restaurant was empty apart from themselves, and the waiters sprang to attention as they entered.

'We'll skip the bar and have a glass of sherry at the table, I think,' Steve said decisively. They were almost overwhelmed with service, one waiter leading them to the best table near the window, looking out on a tremendous vista of mountain peaks, shading from green to purple to a dense black as the last of the day abandoned them, another bringing sherry and the inevitable *tapas*, yet another skimming over with the menu.

'This is like being on stage!' Nicole whispered crossly.

He smiled. 'It's early and they're bored. But you're

right, in a way. We're their entertainment. They will be working out the nature of our relationship, you can bet. They've probably concluded that I'm a disreputable married man, and you're my secretary whom I'm softening up for seduction.'

'They'll be giving you C-minus for technique,' she retorted, forgetting her pious intention to hold her tongue. 'You aren't kissing my neck, or putting your hand on my knee under the table! Perhaps you should put an end to their speculation and tell them we aren't lovers, but jailer and prisoner.'

He spread both hands palms upwards on the tablecloth.

'Oh, really? Where are the handcuffs? I would have thought you'd have had enough drama for one day,' he said unconcernedly. He summoned one of the waiters from the clutch who were hovering nearby. 'I think I shall have the *zarzuela*, with rice. How about you, Nicole? Oh, sorry—I forgot. You said you weren't hungry.'

She looked down at the table, but not quickly enough to hide the baleful expression in her eyes.

'Oh, come on,' he said. 'You *are* hungry, aren't you? You always are, although heaven knows where you put it. You might as well order something. There's very little to be gained by starving yourself.'

'The condemned woman ate a hearty dinner,' she said wryly. 'Oh, all right. I'll have a plain grilled steak and salad. Nothing else.'

It was the height of absurdity that a short time after he had discovered her in the act of trying to filch information from his office they should be sitting here eating dinner together, and Nicole could not help thinking that it was precisely this quality of unpredictability about Steve which unnerved her. He could be fastidiously rude or unpleasant if she offended him, or he could just as easily laugh in her face. He was cruel to the point of ruthlessness at times, but he was equally capable of surprising consideration—as now, because he must have realised before she had herself that, unless she had something to eat, she would flake out from nervous exhaustion.

Nicole disposed of the steak and salad even before he finished his *zarzuela*—an appetising stew of mixed fish—and she had two glasses of the excellent local white wine. Nor did she protest when he ordered *crema Catalana* to follow. As they ate, he conversed lightly about uncontroversial subjects—food, local customs and places of interest—which allowed her to participate as much or as little as she chose. By the time the coffee arrived she was feeling distinctly nervous again. This approach had not put her at her ease, nor did she fool herself it was intended to, and she thought she could have coped better with the glacial, contemptuous Steve who had faced her across his office. At least with him she knew where she stood. Now, she was so confused and disorientated that she feared she would be drained of all powers of resistance when he moved in for the kill—as she was sure he would.

It was dark when they emerged into the car park, a still, warm, perfect night, alive with stars, the dark peaks no more than silent outlines against the indigo sky. A romantic setting—but far from romantic for her, Nicole thought as she slid into the passenger seat of the Mercedes once more. She sensed he was a passionate man with a keen, sensual appreciation of women—a connoisseur. But a romantic? Never, she thought.

He didn't speak at all as he drove, but as they crested the last hill and saw the bay of Castello far below them, its lights a circlet of pearls strung around the dark harbour, she could keep quiet no longer.

'We're going to Peurto de Castello,' she said. 'This road doesn't lead anywhere else.'

'My, you're quick,' he gibed softly. 'Where else did you

think we were going, Nicole? Had you expected me to dump you in the sea, wearing a pair of concrete shoes? You want to get home tonight, don't you?'

Home. The blessed peace of her cottage, with the door shut behind her, sheltering her against all the horrors of this traumatic day! She wanted it more than she could have ever adequately expressed, and it had seemed like an unattainable haven.

'Yes, but——' she began.

'Don't quibble, Nicole,' he said, cutting off her protests firmly. 'If I had slung you out of my office, who knows what you would have done, in that state of mind. I doubt you were fit to drive this road.'

'Your concern for my safety is somewhat misplaced,' she muttered. 'Why should you care if I ended up at the bottom of a ravine? Don't tell me I'd be on your conscience, because if I believed that, I'd believe anything!'

Busy negotiating the steeply twisting descent, he didn't spare her a glance.

'You can't keep it up, can you?' he said. 'It's been an education watching you trying to tread carefully, trying to be polite and subdued and well behaved, but every now and then a flash of temper or a snide little remark breaks through the veneer. You know it would be politic to keep on the right side of me, but you can't quite manage it. Poor Nicole!'

She reacted swiftly against the mocking innuendo of the last two words.

'Save your pity—I don't need it. I'm prepared to take the consequences for what I did—whatever they might be. I just wish you would tell me what you've decided to do, and get on with it.'

The car's smoothly sprung suspension bumped gently over the cobbles as he drew up outside the cottage. Switching off the engine, he left one hand resting on the wheel as he turned to face her.

'I'll tell you what I've decided when I'm good and ready, and consider you need to know. In the meantime, cultivate a little patience. Do nothing for a day or so. Work on your suntan. Swim. Shop. The full tourist bit—you know?'

She sighed.

'But I'm not a tourist, as you well know. If I were, this situation would not have arisen,' she pointed out wearily. 'Sunstyle will expect me to——'

'The hell with Sunstyle!' he exploded abruptly. 'Right now you're taking instructions from me—until further notice. That's the price of your freedom. And *don't* try to sidestep me by turning yourself in to the police. Unless and until I report what happened, they'll know nothing about it, and care even less.'

He got out of the car, opened the door at her side, and waited as she fumbled in her pocket for the key and slotted it into the lock.

'There's just one thing . . .' she began.

'Oh?' He waited expectantly, looking down at her, not exactly smiling, but with a suggestion of amusement hovering at the corners of his mouth.

'My car. It's in a car park in Figueras,' she said shortly.

'Ah——' he exhaled a slow, theatrical sigh. 'How disappointing. I hoped you were going to say how sorry you were for causing me so much bother. And perhaps thank me for having dealt so leniently with you. It just goes to show how mistaken one can be, doesn't it?'

She looked steadily into his eyes that hardened as they held hers, tightening every line of his face and wiping out the memory of his previous thoughtfulness.

'I'll wager there isn't one shred of penitence in you, Nicole,' he said harshly. 'Shame at having been caught out, anger at yourself, and at me, regret for your own folly. But remorse? No! I ought to wring your neck.'

He looked every bit as though he could, his face grim and
dark in the shadows cast by the tall houses, his mouth a thin
line and his body taut with scorn. She did not move, didn't
shrink an inch, and her very refusal to be cowed was a
gauntlet flung at his feet. In some dark, unexplored part of
herself, she wanted his hands to close around her throat;
physical contact, even in the guise of pain, would have been
welcome, and a minor victory for her. But he triumphed by
declining to touch her, and after a long, strained moment of
hesitation she dropped her gaze to the floor, withdrawing
the challenge.

'I'll arrange to have the car sent over,' he said quite
casually, as though bored by the entire business. 'But don't
go anywhere without letting me know. Understood?'

'*Sí, señor. Comprendo,*' she said, turning the key in the
lock. 'Thank you for the dinner. Thank you for not
wringing my unworthy neck!'

The moon, now directly overhead above the rooftops,
allowed her to catch the glimmer of a promise in his
eyes.

'Some other time,' he said.

Alone at last, Nicole locked the door from inside and
leaned exhaustedly against it for a second or two before
dragging herself wearily upstairs to her bedroom.

Tonight, she found to her dismay, she did not
particularly like herself. She did not feel proud of anything
she had done, and was amazed at the foolish, impulsive
streak which had motivated her actions. She had behaved
wrong-headedly and irresponsibly, and what worried her
most of all was wondering whether, if she had been
successful, she would have been chuckling with glee and
self-congratulation. Because, succeed or fail, it would still
have been a deplorable thing to do.

She stripped off the chain-store skirt and jacket—her
disguise, she thought distastefully, dropping them on the

floor—and crawled beneath the cool cotton sheets of her bed. She told herself that Steve was still, beneath all that new moral rectitude, the man who had caused all their misfortunes. But it didn't help. She still ached with regret for the briefly kindled desire he would never again allow himself to have for her, and more for his respect, which she was afraid she had lost for ever.

Nicole had never endured two days which passed as slowly as those which followed. He had immobilised her by not immediately sending back her car, but even if she had had transport, she would have been reluctant to go out viewing the few remaining villas she had not seen. If she had, he would surely hear about it, and he had told her emphatically to do nothing. She was very much conscious that she was on probation, and would be pounced on if she stepped out of line. But she was far too restless and disturbed to relax into the spurious role of tourist.

Most of the time she spent sitting on her patio, writing up her report. Surely he could not fault her for that, even if he knew, and she felt an obligation to discharge the duty with which she had been entrusted. Steve had told her he had not been planning to take over the agency, and it was crazy, when all logic and her own suspicions pointed to that as the only answer—but she believed him.

The report finished, Nicole walked slowly down the steep, cobbled street towards the harbour, deep in thought. She saw, now, what she had to do, and the weight that had bowed her shoulders for two agonising days lifted suddenly as her mind cleared. She sat down at a table outside the Bar Nautico and ordered a coffee, and now, the empty chairs next to hers were occupied by two ghosts. Not only Teddy, enjoying his cigar and Fundador, but Steve, with his hard, interrogative stare and softly authoritative voice were both at her side.

She took out a scrap of paper from her handbag and drafted out a letter telling Peter what she had done, and of the results of her folly. At the end of it, she tendered her resignation. It was up to him whether or not he accepted it, but she owed him the truth . . . or at least, seventy-five per cent of it. He did not need to know about her ill-judged seduction scene in Steve's office, but all the rest was there, including the fact that she did not know whether any action was to be taken against her. She had put her future on the line, but Peter had a right to decide if he chose to carry on employing an idiot with criminal tendencies!

It would not have been accurate to say she felt happier as she retraced her steps to the cottage. She was full of regrets, and a painful sense of loss. But she was buoyed up by the certainty that this was the first decent, honest thing she had done in days, and at last she thought she could face herself without distaste.

The telephone was ringing stridently as she let herself in, and Nicole's heart began to thump with uncomfortable regularity. Could this be Steve, and was she finally to know what her sentence was?

But the voice that crackled over the line was Heather's, and the Sunstyle secretary sounded harassed and agitated.

'Thank goodness I've caught you!' she said. 'Can you get back as quickly as possible? Mr Delamere says don't drive up, book a flight right away. He wants you at head office immediately.'

The painful thumping in Nicole's chest increased as an awful suspicion gripped her. Could it be that Peter already knew what she had to tell him? If so, there was only one way he could have come by that knowledge!

Don't imagine you're going to get off scot-free, Steve had warned ominously. But surely, he wouldn't . . .?

Oh yes, he would, Nicole thought grimly, and a whole army of mistrustful suspicions came marching back.

'What's all this about, Heather?' she asked, trying to keep her voice light. 'Am I on the carpet?'

'Not so far as I know. But there's the most awful flap on, and none of us really knows what's happening. The board have been closeted in the boardroom most of yesterday and today, and Peter's secretary is as tight as a clam about it. Obviously, her lips are sealed. All I have is a message that you're to get back, pronto!'

Nicole was thoughtful as she replaced the receiver. Surely the 'awful flap' that Heather had described, with secretive meetings of the full board, and an embargo on all discussion of the agenda, was not a result of her misdeeds. It simply was not that important, she knew. But something was going on, clearly, and she must be involved in it if Peter had ordered her back to base so promptly.

She had the grace to wonder if she had perhaps misjudged Steve, immediately jumping to the conclusion that he was behind it, and wondered if she would ever break the ingrained habit of blaming him for whatever went wrong in her life. At least she owed him the courtesy of explaining that she was not slipping away behind his back, because she did not have the guts to stay and face the music, and she put through a call to his office in Figueras.

Señora Roig was politely distant. No, Señor Rodriguez was not in the office. In fact, he was not in Figueras at all today. She could not get in touch with him, and had no idea when he would be back. Could she take a message?

Nicole did not believe a confidential secretary at that level was not fully cognisant of her chief's movements—she was simply protecting him from a woman she saw as a nuisance. Unconvinced that her message would even get through, she thanked her and rang off. She could not find the number of his Figueras apartment listed in the directory, so after a moment's hesitation she rang Vistamar, thinking that she could perhaps speak to Lacey.

She imagined the telephone ringing in the shady hall with its floor of travertine marble, and then told herself not to be fanciful. There were extensions all over the house, and most probably the housekeeper would answer the one in the kitchen.

But the voice which answered, although female, was not that of the middle-aged housekeeper she had met briefly when she delivered Lacey there. It was the voice of a mature young woman, poised, cool and self-assured.

Nicole was a little thrown, but she recovered herself quickly.

'I wanted to get in touch with Steve—Señor Rodriguez —but I understand he isn't in his office today,' she explained.

'He's certainly not here,' the woman's voice said positively. 'I'm his sister, and *I* haven't seen him since last weekend. Have you tried his apartment in Figueras?'

'I couldn't. I don't know the number, and I can't find it in the book,' Nicole said.

Juana Rodriguez laughed.

'It isn't in the book. My brother is very guarded with that number, and if you don't know it, I'm afraid I can't tell you,' she said. 'It's unlikely you would find him there at this time of day, anyhow.'

Nicole scratched her head. Get the first flight available, Peter had instructed, but she absolutely had to make it clear to Steve that she had not run away in a panic. She decided that she would trust Juana rather than Señora Roig. According to Lacey, she, too, had felt the rough edge of Steve's decisions.

'Could you please give him a message from me? It's very important that he gets it. Say Nicole rang, that my directors have ordered me to fly to London today, but I will be coming back.'

'Of course, I'll tell him,' Juana said unhesitantly. 'Don't

worry—I'll leave word all over the place, even with that Gorgon who guards his office. *Adios,* Nicole. Have a good flight.'

She sounded sharp, witty and yet sympathetic, and Nicole reflected that there was one member of the Rodriguez family she would have liked, had they met. But she had no time to waste and, after checking that there was a flight available, she swiftly packed a few essentials in an overnight bag and arranged for a taxi to take her to the airport.

It was a scheduled night flight to Gatwick, on which she was lucky to get the last remaining seat, but it landed her in the early morning, bleary-eyed and sleepless. There was no way she was going to face whatever was happening at the office looking like a crumpled, wrung-out dishcloth, although by the time she reached town it was almost time for the working day to begin. She took the Tube to her flat, showered, washed her hair and put on her smartest suit, a grey pencil skirt and long-line, single-breasted jacket. Pinning up her hair into its businesslike French pleat, she made herself drink a cup of tea and force down a slice of toast. More than that she could not have stomached, even if she had had the time.

The atmosphere at Sunstyle was so thick it could have been sliced with a knife. Every office was buzzing with secretive conversations which tailed off into sudden, tense silences. Nicole reported her presence to Sally, Peter's secretary, and then perched uneasily on the edge of her desk, watching the comings and goings along the corridor. Heather kept the kettle continuously on the boil, making coffee for anyone who came in, and speculation mounted as the minutes ticked away.

'There's a rumour that we're going out of business,' one of the accounts clerks muttered gloomily. 'Bang goes my mortgage, if that's true! I can only just keep up the payments as it is!'

'That must be nonsense! Healthy companies don't go out of business, just like that!' Heather said briskly.

'No, but they can be taken over,' someone else put in darkly. 'Then you can bet your life that some of us would be out of a job.'

They all looked at Nicole, who was closest among them to the seat of power, who had consultations with the directors and access to some of the forward planning. She shrugged helplessly.

'I don't know any more than you do—and I've been out of the country, remember. But there was no talk of that kind before I left. We're supposed to be expanding . . . and there are usually some indications if a company is being stalked for a takeover.'

A slow, sarcastic hand-clap from the doorway made them all turn to see Adrian Delamere standing there. His boyishly handsome face wore an ironic smile, he had his briefcase in one hand, a pile of assorted belongings tucked under the other arm, and although his assertively lecherous gaze did its usual study of Nicole's legs, there was a defeated petulance about him.

'Very clever, Nicole!' he applauded jeeringly. 'But in this case, the hunter kept close to the ground and didn't spring until the last moment.'

She stared at him, disbelievingly.

'It's true, then?' she demanded, and he nodded.

'True enough. You've all got a new boss, as from today, and I wish you joy of him. Personally, I'm not sticking around to kowtow to the new management.'

His eyes travelled hotly up the length of Nicole's body in the manner she had always disliked, but tried to ignore.

'I wouldn't be in your shoes for the world, darling,' he said. 'You're going to be the one running the Spanish thing, and this predator will be right behind you, breathing down your neck. We all know what Latins are like, don't we, so keep your knickers up, won't you, my love?'

Nicole did not have time to tell him not to be so vulgar, as, with a final jaunty wave of defiance, he wheeled out of the room, leaving them all speechless. Seconds later, he popped his head back round the door, grinning fiendishly. 'Silly me—I forgot to tell you his name,' he said with a shrug. 'But you know him, of course, Nicole. He certainly knows *you*. It's Esteban Rodriguez—and may you be very happy together!'

CHAPTER SIX

A STUNNED silence followed Adrian's abrupt, dramatic departure, and then babel broke out, everyone talking at once, speculating on their own and the company's future, bombarding Nicole with questions.

She shook her head firmly, tight-lipped.

'The less I say about Esteban Rodriguez, the better it will be for all concerned,' she said tersely. 'Heather—can I have the loan of your typewriter for precisely two minutes?

'Of course.' The secretary looked on, puzzled, as Nicole slotted in a sheet of paper and briskly typed out a few short lines. 'What are you doing? You're not . . . oh, no, Nicole, don't!'

Nicole allowed herself a grim smile.

'That's right. I'm following Adrian's example,' she said. 'I know I haven't agreed with him too often in the past, but on this occasion I'm in full accord. I don't want to work for the new management, either.'

She folded up her letter of resignation—not the full, detailed explanation she had prepared for Peter, which she now felt was no longer necessary, but a simple statement of her wish to terminate her employment. Then, ignoring the remonstrances of her distressed colleagues, she rang through to Peter's secretary and told her she would like to see Mr Delamere as soon as it was convenient.

'You must be clairvoyant,' Sally exclaimed. 'I was about to ring you. You're wanted in the boardroom immediately.'

Nicole took a deep breath. All the dreams and ambitions she had nursed since the day she entered this building as a green young student ended here. Her throat was tight with regret, and unshed tears were only just held at bay as she walked firmly along the corridor. She hated this more than anything she had ever had to do, but she could not work for Steve Rodriguez.

Nor, of course, would he require her to. Here, she was sure, was the punishment he had warned her that he would mete out, and no doubt he had known all along what form he had intended it to take. How could she have believed him, even for a moment, when he assured her he had no plans to run the Spanish agency? Leopards' spots were indelibly printed, and once a cheat, always a cheat, she thought despairingly.

Nicole tapped on the boardroom door, hoping that she need encounter only Peter, and not the entire board. This was going to be hard enough, without everyone firing questions at her—questions which she had no heart to answer.

The long, narrow room with its oval table, olive green carpet and discreetly netted windows obscuring the bustle of the street beyond them was empty save for the figure of one man, standing at the far end of the table, hands resting lightly on the back of a chair. Nicole's sigh of relief died in her throat, for it was not Peter Delamere but Steve Rodriguez who faced her, his expression calmly inscrutable, with just the faintest question in the granite eyes.

She did not hesitate, but walked quickly across the room and tossed the letter on to the table in front of him, without a word. In equal silence he picked it up, unfolded it, and scanned it swiftly, not a flicker of response showing on his hard-lined face.

They stared at one another for a full half-minute, and her nerve faltered first—as it always did, she thought bitterly.

'I assume that's required of me, so I've saved you the trouble of giving me my notice,' she said, as coldly as possible.

He slid the letter back towards her along the polished table-top.

'Then you can just take that back, as I had no intention of firing you, and I won't accept your resignation,' he told her, his tone more than matching hers.

She could not mask her astonishment at this, but continued to stare at him uncomprehendingly.

'You *have* to accept it. I don't want to work for you,' she said bluntly.

He treated her insistence with an annoying disregard.

'Tut, tut! Nicole! Where's your loyalty?' he challenged lightly. 'All evaporated, has it? Gone up in smoke? And you had me believing you were such a conscientious, highly motivated employee.'

'My loyalty was to Sunstyle and Peter Delamere,' she retorted curtly. 'I can't transfer it as easily as you seem to think. Nor can I work for an employer I can't trust. You told me you had no plans with regard to the agency.'

'Nor did I. You should listen more carefully. I usually say what I mean—no more nor less,' he said, looking down at her angry face, quite unmoved and almost disdainful. 'I wouldn't waste my time competing with Sunstyle for a property-letting agency, which was what you accused me of. Taking over the parent company is another matter altogether.'

Nicole sniffed suspiciously.

'I still maintain that's hair-splitting,' she protested. 'However, it's all purely academic whether you told me a version of the truth or not. I won't work for you, and you can't force me. My letter is on the table.'

She turned and walked away defiantly, her back straight and her head high. He let her put her hand on the doorknob before he said quietly, but in a voice of such chilling authority that it caused the fine hairs to rise on the nape of her neck, 'If you walk through that door, you had better face the fact that you may never work in the travel business again.'

She stiffened, but did not turn around.

'You'd stoop to that, wouldn't you?' she said contemptuously. 'You'd use your influence to prevent me from getting a similar position.'

Her scorn did not appear to trouble him unduly.

'It wouldn't be too difficult,' he agreed. 'A word here and there . . . no one wants an employee with a shady reputation in a position of trust. You could also have a criminal record which, while it would hardly merit extradition, might make it awkward for you to return to Spain at some future date without facing charges. Turn around, Nicole,' he added sharply, rapping out the last three words. 'I prefer to talk to a person's face, rather than the back of her head.'

Very slowly, after a fractional hesitation, she turned, and there was bitterness in the eyes she raised to his, as well as anger.

'You're despicable!' she said fiercely.

He shrugged.

'No, I'm not. Merely practical. You may have made one mistake, which I shall attribute to over-zealousness, but you're a good executive. Peter Delamere thinks very highly of you, and I'm impressed by your past records. Why should I allow you to leave and work for one of Sunstyle's competitors? That would be injudicious of me, wouldn't it?'

How she hated that softly incisive voice which remained level and superbly controlled, when she was full of a seething frustration, wild enough to make her want to kill!

'After all,' he continued with the same insidious smoothness, 'it isn't as if I were condemning you to some awful fate. You will do the job Peter had planned for you all along—launching the Spanish agency and then overseeing it, while retaining some overall responsibilities you already possess. Naturally, there will be a commensurate salary increase.'

'But I can't——' Nicole began hotly. Then the door clicked behind her and, half turning, she saw Peter Delamere. He looked tired and harassed, but a smile creased his face as he looked at her.

'Ah—Nicole. Sorry to have to drag you back at such short notice. I gather Steve has been explaining the new set-up to you?'

'Actually, Peter, I've had to use a certain amount of persuasion,' Steve said smoothly. 'Nicole seemed to think we wouldn't require her services any further. I think I've just about convinced her she's indispensable.'

'Not require her services? What nonsense!' Peter said warmly. 'You'd have to look a long way, Steve, to find anyone with Nicole's potential.'

Nicole's glance sped between the two men. What was all this 'Steve' and 'Peter' stuff? she wondered with increasing bewilderment. The two men were behaving like friends, rather than a company director who has just been ruthlessly taken over, and his merciless conqueror. In confused desperation, she appealed to her erstwhile boss.

'Peter, I'm sure you'll understand. I've always worked for you, and I'm not sure that I can adapt to the new management structure.'

'Nicole, you'll *still* work for me,' he assured her. 'At least, in the sense that I shall still be managing director of Sunstyle. We'll be an independent company within the body of a larger group, and, while we shall have the Rodriguez resources behind us, our basic policy won't change.' He studied her doubtful face worriedly. 'For heaven's sake, Nicole, don't *you* desert me, now,' he begged. 'It's bad enough having my own brother playing dirty tricks behind my back, without losing my key personnel in addition!'

Nicole's blue eyes widened incredulously. She looked at Steve, but nothing in his dark face enlightened her—he merely raised his eyebrows a centimetre, throwing the question back. It was to Peter that he spoke.

'I haven't told her all that,' he said gravely. 'I thought you would prefer to do so yourself. What happened within your organisation is in the past, and concerned your brother . . . and Nicole's colleague, so I thought the explanation would come better from you.'

'Yes. Thank you—I'm grateful for that.' Peter turned away, and she saw he was visibly struggling for control over some emotion which was still a mystery to her, but obviously had something to do with Adrian. And she had to admit that Steve displayed considerable tact, leaving the other man to his private battle without drawing any attention to it.

He picked up the letter from the table and handed it back to Nicole.

'It's your decision, ultimately,' he said quietly, and Nicole was sure that only she heard the warning note in his voice. 'But I think I made my position clear. I'm staying at the Dorchester. Perhaps you'll give me a ring, either this evening, or tomorrow morning. Don't leave it too late. I've a plane to catch.'

That afternoon, Nicole caught a bus out into the peaceful Kentish countryside to St Anthony's Hospice. She did not phone first to say she was coming, knowing that the surprise of the unexpected visit would give her mother even greater pleasure, but she was taken aback by the gravity of Sister Cornelia's usually cheerful face.

'She's taken a turn for the worse,' she told Nicole without preamble. 'I wanted to send for you, but she wouldn't hear of it—said you had some new job responsibilities, and we weren't to upset you. I've humoured her so far, but I wouldn't have gone along with it for much longer.'

Nicole was aware of a cold, lonely sensation, like frozen fingers squeezing her heart. She clung to whatever vestige of hope she could dredge up.

'She's had bad spells before and rallied,' she said hopefully. 'Could it happen again?'

The Sister laid a kindly, practical hand on her arm.

'My dear, I think we are only talking about a very limited time span now. The rest of the summer, at most. But you may be assured we won't let her suffer, and I'll send for you so that you can be with her when the end does come.'

Nicole nodded, forcing down the choking sensation that made her want to cry, and for the rest of the afternoon she sat at her mother's bedside. Lorraine slept for most of the time, the increasingly large dose of pain-killing drugs making her comatose, but Nicole was saddened by her frailty, and the grey pallor of the once fine, fair skin.

She did awake once, and her smile was radiantly happy as she caught sight of her daughter at her bedside. They talked for a short time, and Lorraine was clearly delighted with her daughter's success, though still fretting about her proximity to Steve Rodriguez.

She need never know the truth about the takeover, Nicole promised herself firmly as she left the hospice that evening. She never read the financial news, so she'd never find out by herself. Nor must any breath of scandal ever come to her ears about what had happened in Spain, no whisper of a cloud over Nicole's future.

She had been troubled and still undecided when she made her journey earlier that afternoon. Undoubtedly, what Peter had told her after Steve left them alone in the boardroom showed up events in a different complexion.

'Adrian was trying to negotiate a merger with Interglobe behind my back,' Peter said, anger and shame mingled in his voice. 'My own brother! Attempting to subvert other board members to work against me . . . we couldn't have held Interglobe off without Rodriguez.'

Nicole was deeply thoughtful for a while. She knew the sort of operation Interglobe ran—huge, skyscraper hotels in resorts they virtually took over, packed with hundreds of people jetted in twice weekly. Maybe there were places where that kind of thing was more appropriate, but she shuddered at the thought of it happening to Puerto de Castello. What was it Steve had said, on that first evening at the Bar Nautico? 'A different hand on the helm . . . a takeover by a bigger, brasher concern . . .' He must have known, even then, must have been wheeling and dealing behind the scenes. He had been right, damn him, and she had been wrong to say it couldn't happen—and that hurt!

'But now you are a part of the Rodriguez empire,' she said slowly. 'You're no longer an independent company, in the sense that you were before.'

Peter smiled.

'There's a price for everything, Nicole,' he said. 'We've been promised a free hand to run Sunstyle our way, so long as the profits are healthy. Steve Rodriguez has personally given me his word on that.'

Nicole's glance was rueful.

'Do you trust his word?'

'I have no reason not to. His reputation is one of being hard, but fair. But we have to prove ourselves within the group, and that's why I need you to see the Spanish side of things through. You done all the groundwork, and you're the right person for the job. Quite honestly, I don't see what objection you can have—unless there's something personal, something between you and him, which you're not telling me about.'

Nicole had remained silent on that, had asked and been granted time to consider her decision. Hard, but fair, she thought, with a grim little laugh. Maybe Steve could afford a moral reputation now, maybe there were few with memories to match her own, who knew how he had started out far less righteously. But what good would it do Peter, now, to know about Steve's dubious past? And he *had* left her own image untarnished by saying nothing to Peter about her misdeeds.

Nicole let herself back into her flat, and after a long, thoughtful pause picked up the receiver and rang the Dorchester, asking to be put through to Mr Rodriguez. Could she have chosen purely for herself, there would have been no price he could have paid which would have made her eat his salt. But she did owe something to Peter, who had shown so much faith in her over the years, and who had surely suffered enough from Adrian's defection. At least she could get the Spanish agency working smoothly for him. And nothing, she vowed fiercely, was going to burden the last months of her mother's life with any further sadness. Lorraine had had more than anyone's natural share, and if nothing else, she would die content.

After that, we'll see, Nicole thought grimly. After that, I don't *care*.

'Rodriguez,' said the calm, dry voice at the other end of the line, and Nicole's heart began to adopt a strange rhythm, quite foreign to its usual measured beat; her palms were clammy, and it cost her an effort to speak in a level, undisturbed tone.

'It's Nicole,' she said, forcing out the words, each one of which demanded every ounce of determination of which she was capable. 'You asked me to phone. I've decided to . . . to accept your offer.'

He made her wait what seemed an inordinate length of time before replying.

'Be at Heathrow Terminal One tomorrow at midday,' he said distantly, reducing to insignificance all the thought and effort, all the heart-searching which had gone into her decision. 'Your flight is already booked.'

Nicole arrived at the airport to find Steve already there, and the formalities of checking in and boarding were easier in his presence than she had ever known them to be. But then, she had never flown first-class before, either; the quiet luxury and extra attentiveness were a new—and, she had to admit, not unpleasant—experience.

When they landed at Gerona and cleared Customs, again with effortless ease, he led her straight out to where the white Mercedes was parked.

'Your car's at Puerto de Castello,' he informed her. 'Don't worry—you'll be mobile again, very shortly.'

'You don't have to drive me there—I can make my own arrangements,' she said. 'I have no wish to inconvenience you.'

'You won't,' he said. 'Get in.'

Nicole settled herself into the passenger seat, consoling herself that in a short space of time he would be gone and she could get on with her work, pretending to the best of her ability that Steve Rodriguez was not ultimately her boss. After all, how much did ordinary employees of multinational concerns ever see of the chairman? All right, so this one lived at least part of the time in Puerto de Castello, but he had said he would not interfere without good reason. She would make very sure not to give him any. Sunstyle's Spanish operation would be managed so well, so efficiently, that he never need concern himself with it. It might be that, now the agency question was settled, and the entire organisation belonged to him, he would trouble her less than he had before.

With this in mind, Nocole felt her spirits lift as the car crested the mountain road and Puerto de Castello lay at her feet. She was back in Spain—the harsh, brilliant sunshine, the baked hills and the vivid, primary colours of sea, sky and flowers were vital to her in a way she had not understood until she was deprived of them. She was off the hook, so far as her escapade at the Rodriguez offices was concerned—at least, so she assumed, although Steve had not said so in as many words. And any minute now she would see the back of the white Mercedes and its owner!

But, instead of driving into the village centre, Steve turned the car the other way, out along the coast road.

'You could have dropped me outside the village,' she protested, a little pulse of alarm beginning to beat at her temple, because he very rarely took any action without thought. Her composure deserted her as they turned up the curving drive to Vistamar. 'Steve! Where are you taking me?'

'It's fairly obvious, isn't it? Don't ask silly questions, Nicole.' He drew the white Mercedes to a neat halt in front of the house, whose white walls gleamed softly in the bright sun, and were reflected in the blue of the swimming pool. The gardens were brilliant with roses and hydrangeas, and trailing pelargoniums dripped scarlet patterns from the walls of the terrace. It had never looked more beautiful, more inviting, and Nicole desperately wanted to get away.

'I decided it would be best if you lived here, at Vistamar, while you are in Spain,' Steve said airily.

'No!' Nicole's cry of protest was swift, instinctive, and came from deep inside her, without reasoned thought. Her hands were clenched, showing the white bones of her knuckles, and an expression of anguish flitted across her face before she was capable of controlling it.

He half turned towards her in the front seat, his arm resting along the steering wheel.

'That's a fine reaction to my offer of hospitality,' he said. 'People don't usually blanch at the prospect of staying here. You'll be more than comfortable, I promise you. You can make use of the computer in the study . . . and the pool. And, since meals will appear in front of you at regular intervals, you'll have more time to work, less to waste on shopping, cooking, and other domestic trivia.'

'I would prefer to stay at the cottage,' Nicole objected stubbornly. 'I've always used the accommodation my clients occupy, as a matter of principle.'

'No doubt, but I'd rather you stayed here and, much as I hate to pull rank, I have to remind you I'm the boss,' he said mildly. 'Anyone I'm not one hundred per cent sure of, I like to have where I can keep an eye on them, and you have this tendency to flee the country when my back is turned.'

She drew in her breath in sharp outrage.

'That's unfair! You *know* why I had to go to London— who better? And I tried my best to get a message through to you, although it wasn't easy, since your secretary was unhelpful, and your phone number in Figueras is guarded as closely as Fort Knox!'

He smiled teasingly, but there was a watchful quality in his eyes as he said, 'I don't give my phone number to all and sundry, because I like my private life to be precisely that. And my secretary had strict instructions not to reveal my whereabouts. When I'm involved in high-level takeover negotiations, I don't want them splashed all over the Press—or revealed to my rivals.'

From the way he looked at her, Nicole knew this was more than just a casual comment. It was too pointed, too direct, with her too obviously its target.

'What exactly are you accusing me of?' she asked, with uneasy resentment.

'Nothing—right now,' he said significantly. 'But one can't be too careful. The finger pointed at Adrian Delamere, but he could have had an accomplice. And then you turned up in my office, clearly up to no good. Can you blame me for having my suspicions?'

At first Nicole was indignant, but, as she thought about it, she realised that what he said was not entirely impossible.

'But surely you don't still believe that I was in league with Adrian?' she protested.

He shook his head.

'You wouldn't be here now, if I did. You'd be pounding the pavements in search of a job. My own judgement, your past records, and all that Peter said about you convinced me that you were not involved.'

'Then why do I have to be here, under your supervision?' she demanded indignantly. 'If you trust me, leave me alone.'

'Did I say I trusted you?' he laughed harshly. 'I believe you are good at your job, and I'm prepared to make use of your expertise. But there's a sense in which I'm not at all sure of you. So you'll stay here, Nicole—for the present, anyhow. If you fulfil your promises, that cottage should soon be occupied by tourists, along with all the other properties on Sunstyle's books, and therefore not available for your use. I've cancelled your tenancy, your car's in the garage, and your personal possessions are already here.'

She gasped at the flagrant effortery of this high-handed treatment.

'You mean to tell me that someone went into my bedroom and messed around with my clothes?' she cried. 'I have to tell you I object most strongly to that!'

'Don't look at me like that,' he said, amused by her shaking anger. 'I didn't personally fold up your smalls—I'm not a lingerie freak, and anyhow I drove straight to Gerona airport after leaving you at the cottage. Relax—my sister moved your stuff, at my request, and no one is more careful of clothes than she is.'

He got out of the car and opened the door for her; like a

sleepwalker, Nicole's limbs moved, not seeming to touch the ground, divorced from reality. There was nothing he could have done to her which hurt as much as this . . . it was ironic, almost laughable, that he could punish her so severely without knowing it.

To be obliged to work for him . . . she had come to terms with that, knowing she must maintain the outward semblance of normality over these next months, for Lorraine's sake. But to have to live here at Vistamar, once her beloved home, was too poignant to bear. To have to pretend, what was worse, that it was just a house, someone else's house, and meant no more to her than that . . .

Nicole squared her shoulders. Pretend she must, if the effort killed her, for Steve Rodriguez held her fate more securely than ever in his hands, now that she was answerable to him—and not only hers, but Peter's, and the rest of her colleagues at Sunstyle. She dared not think of how he might react if he were to discover now that not only was she Teddy Walton's stepdaughter, but that she had deceived him about her identity.

The hot sun beat down on her back and shoulders, but she shuddered, looked up at the man at her side, and caught him watching her. Not smiling, simply looking, the slate-dark eyes asking of her something unknown, and therefore unanswerable.

'What are we waiting for now?' he enquired. 'Were you expecting me to conform to the Spanish stereotype and say *"está es su casa"*?'

Nicole was gripped by an unreasoning fear, a blind, juvenile panic which she told herself was no more than the workings of her conscience, uneasy with this element of deception. Drawing heavily on the half-forgotten experience of her drama club days, she shrugged and favoured him with a dazzling, open smile.

'I always did consider that a puzzling expression,' she

responded lightly. *Está es su casa,* indeed! And so it was once and still should have been! 'If you really were so foolish as to offer me your delightful house, you can be certain I should take you up on the offer, and I shouldn't be in any hurry to give it back to you.'

He showed every appearance of giving her words weighty consideration.

'What I give, I don't usually ask to be returned,' he replied steadily. 'On the other hand, what I take, I make a habit of keeping. Shall we go inside?'

He closed the car door and then, his hand under her elbow, turned her towards the terrace. The pressure was barely perceptible, yet a sharp thrill sang painfully along the nerves of her upper arm, and she knew that in spite of everything she could never again be immune to the touch of his hand. The warm palm and the cool fingers, the steel-hard eyes and the shrewd, manipulative brain whose bidding they all did, continued to hold in thrall the intimate core of her deepest woman's self.

Free? How had she ever been crazy enough to think she could be free of him? He was entwined in the fabric of her life, always had been, and always would be. Any freedom she tried to convince herself she possessed was no more than a vain illusion. The reality was otherwise, and as she walked up the short flight of steps to her old, much-loved home, Nicole could do no less than acknowledge it.

CHAPTER SEVEN

STEVE did not remain at Vistamar long after depositing Nicole there. He had meetings scheduled for the whole of the afternoon, he told her, and work to catch up on which had been accumulating in his absence.

'In fact, I very much doubt I'll be back before the weekend,' he said. 'But Señora Alvarez, my housekeeper, will look after you, and Lacey is here—somewhere. Juana may drop in. Just treat the place as your home.'

Nicole tried to ignore the irony of this as she watched him disappear down the drive. Oddly enough, she was helped by the fact that although from the outside Vistamar looked much the same, internally just about everything had changed.

Somehow, she had foolishly imagined it as it had been in her day, with Lorraine's chintz soft covers vying with the cane tables and chairs Teddy had fondly thought of as intrinsically Spanish. The only cane furniture now in evidence was on the terrace, and there was nothing chintzy-flowery at all about the décor. It echoed the colours of the landscape all around . . . white on more white, with touches of gold, olive green and deep, ultramarine blue, tiles of terracotta and umber and deep-pile rugs of blue and ivory. The furniture was stylishly modern, and she had to admit the effect was spacious and relaxing.

Señora Alvarez ushered Nicole upstairs to her room, and there she found Lacey, who was touchingly pleased to see her.

'It will be great to have someone else here who's not Spanish!' she said. 'I won't be so outnumbered! I was pleased when I heard you'd be staying. It's so *boring* here!'

Nicole smiled, and looked out of the window from where she had a stunning view out across the bay, the village, and the sea beyond. Directly beneath her balcony, the pool sparkled invitingly.

'Let's swim,' she suggested. Several days of concentrated work, travel and worry had made her disinclined to do anything but take easy what remained of today, and Steve *had* said she was to treat the house as her home. Why shouldn't she take him at his word?

'All right.' Lacey had a pile of pop posters in her hand. 'I just came to take some of these down, because I'd forgotten them. My father said we should let you have this room, as it's the biggest.'

'I wouldn't have wanted to turn you out of your room!' Nicole protested. 'That was quite unnecessary.'

'Oh—hey!' Lacey shrugged. 'I hate this house, anyway, so what does it matter which room I sleep in? So long as I have Duran on the walls—I couldn't live without Simon le Bon!'

Nicole dropped her overnight bag on the floor.

'I won't deprive you of Simon, as well as your room,' she laughed. 'But why do you hate Vistamar, Lacey? I used——' She bit her tongue as the mistake almost slipped out. 'I mean, I would have thought it was the nearest thing to Paradise.'

'Oh, gosh!' Lacey's eyes rolled ceilingwards, and her complaint ended up as a mournful wail. 'I hate the whole place, not just the house! It's so *boring*, there's nothing to do, and I don't have any friends, and everybody speaks Spanish, except me! No one wants me here, they're all too busy—I want to go home! But I can't, because no one's there. Mom's still off somewhere with Don, and she hasn't even phoned for a week!'

She sniffed miserably. Nicole remembered the glum,

troublesome girl who had travelled through France with her, and wondered if this were the first time that Lacey had opened up to anyone about how unhappy she was.

'Oh, Lacey! Have you told your father you feel like this?' she asked, and the girl shook her head.

'I can't. He's hardly ever here, and when he is, he's always brought work home to do,' she moaned. 'Besides, I know he'd be only too glad to send me back to the States, only he can't, can he? He's lumbered with me, whether he likes it or not!'

Nicole's lips pursed slightly, and she thought someone should tell Steve to make a better job of hiding his reluctance to have his daughter staying with him. Deep down, she recoiled from being the one to undertake this hazardous mission.

Fortunately, Steve would not be back until the weekend, so it was a problem she did not have to face immediately.

'What about that swim?' she suggested.

'Sure. I've got two swimsuits with me. Trouble is, both of them make me look like a dinosaur!' Lacey said self-deprecatingly. 'Come and help me choose the least awful.'

Whatever faults Steve's daughter had, vanity was not one of them, Nicole thought, smiling to herself as she followed the girl to her new room.

The smile froze on her lips as they reached the door, for this was the room that had once been hers, the one she had chosen when they first moved into Vistamar. It was a small, oddly shaped room with a double aspect, one window facing the sea, and the other overlooking the tennis courts and the peaceful pine forests clothing the steep hills behind the house.

Nicole pressed a hand to her mouth, thanking God that Steve had made Lacey vacate her original room. Otherwise, she might have had to occupy this one herself, and that would truly have been more than she could bear.

It was fortunate that Lacey, with the egotism of youth, did not notice anything amiss, but grumbled on about the dire state of her wardrobe, the shortcomings of her figure, and the awfulness of life in general.

A day might come, Nicole thought, when she could face this room with equanimity, when she could live at peace with the ghost of her fourteen-year-old self, reconciling the good memories with the bad. But that day had not come yet, and until it did there was only so much that she could take.

Over the days and weeks that followed, Nicole threw herself into her work with a wholeheartedness which left her scant time to brood over any problems not connected with it.

Juana Rodriguez turned up at Vistamar a few days after Nicole moved in. She careered up the drive in a racy little Citroën with the sun-top rolled down, and jerked to a stop at the very last moment, snatching on the handbrake.

'It's my aunt Juana,' Lacey observed from the terrace, where she was drinking Coke, eating chocolate, and reading a teenage magazine for the sixtieth time. 'She drives like there's no tomorrow.'

Juana was darker than her brother, slim, feline and energetic. Her long hair was fashionably tousled into a style which suggested she had just got out of bed, and her eyes were not grey, like Steve's, but the pale amber of a good *fino* sherry. She wore pink and white striped cropped trousers, a baggy white overblouse with a wide leather belt slung around the hips, and a mid-calf cotton coat of vivid cerise. A king's ransom of gold jewellery, obviously the real thing, hung gleaming around her tanned neck, her wrists, and from her ears. Oddly enough, this bizarre combination worked perfectly—on her, at least.

'So you're Nicole,' she grinned, showing sharp, perfect

white teeth. 'I gather you're working for my brother now?
Join the club. I warn you, he's a slave-driver. Only
workaholics need apply. Are you one?'

Nicole smiled cautiously. Her instinct about Juana had
been right; she knew already that they would get on, but it
was easy to see that hers was not a restful presence.

'I enjoy my job, and I do it to the best of my ability,' she
answered. 'But I believe the rest of my life, outside work, is
my own business.'

Juana grimaced.

'I've news for you. Not here, it isn't,' she hinted darkly.
Divesting herself of the coat, she flung her lean frame into a
chair and sniffed at the contents of the jug on the table.
'What's this? Sangria? Isn't there any gin?'

The housekeeper, having heard the car and being
conversant with Juana's likes and dislikes, was already
hurrying out with bottle, ice-bucket and glasses on a
tray.

'*Salud, amor y pesetas!*' Juana said, raising her glass and
taking a gulp. 'Aren't you going to join me, Nicole?'

'I think I'll stick with this.' Nicole refilled her glass with
sangria, and Juana regarded her with lively curiosity over
the frosty rim of her own.

'So, how do you get on with Steve?' she demanded
uninhibitedly. 'He doesn't bring every new executive to
stay at Vistamar, so do I take it that you and he have a
special relationship?'

Nicole only just managed to avoid spilling sangria down
the front of her white sundress.

'Certainly not!' she contradicted emphatically. 'It isn't
like that at all.'

The alert, humorous amber eyes continued to regard her,
unconvinced, from beneath neatly plucked, finely arched
dark brows, and she was obliged to expand her protest into
an explanation of sorts.

'I think he believed it would be easier for me to get the agency working properly if I could devote my attention to it full time. Living here, I don't have to shop, or cook.'

Lacey, although apparently still immersed in her magazine, had a watchful attitude about her which suggested that she wasn't missing any of the implications of this adult conversation. Nicole wished Juana were less forthright. She didn't want the girl getting any wrong ideas about Steve and herself.

'Hm,' Juana said consideringly. 'He never brings his ladies here, so I wouldn't know if there's a current one. In my opinion, it's high time he married again, but he says he's cured of that disease, once and for all.'

Lacey's chair scraped on the flagstones of the terrace as she rose abruptly and stalked into the house. Juana looked momentarily surprised, then said, 'Oh dear—I suppose that was a little tactless of me.'

Nicole thought that was the understatement of the year, but it was hardly her place to say so.

'You *were* talking about her mother and father,' was all she said, mildly.

Juana leaned forward and set down her glass.

'Let me tell you something,' she said, with quiet urgency. 'My brother is no saint, and he and I disagree often and violently. But he didn't deserve Sonia, and he's well rid of her. She was always a two-timing bitch, and all she wants now is as much money as she can extort from him. Lord knows, he gives her plenty, but she resents the fact that she's not entitled to half of all he has—because the bulk of his money was not made until after their divorce. Nor has she all that much time for Lacey—the poor kid is just a lever to manipulate Steve, and has been since the day she was born. Steve, for all his faults, does *care* about the child.'

She poured herself another drink.

'Sorry if my language upsets you. I'm used to speaking plainly,' she said.

'It doesn't upset me in the least,' Nicole said truthfully. 'I'm not so sure Lacey's mature enough to take it, though. And somehow I find it difficult to imagine anyone manipulating your brother.'

Juana gave a snort.

'He doesn't leave himself vulnerable on many fronts, these days. But Lacey *is* his daughter.'

To Nicole, the concept of the almighty, influential, armour-plated Steve Rodriguez being in any way vulnerable was elusive to the point of invisibility. Was there a chink in the armour? She remembered the occasional, fleeting note of bitterness when his marriage was mentioned, and a suggestion of grief, quickly concealed, when he spoke of the death of his parents. If there were areas where he could be hurt, they were buried too deeply to be easily divined.

'If he cares about Lacey, he should let her know it a little,' she pointed out. 'She's convinced he doesn't want her, and never has.'

Juana shrugged expressive shoulders, the gold chains clinking in orchestration as she moved.

'Naturally she thinks that—it's what Sonia has been instilling into her since she was old enough to crawl out of her playpen,' she said. 'The trouble with Steve is that he thinks if something is the truth it should become self-evident, and he shouldn't have to lower himself to persuade or convince. Lacey will eventually realise that everything Sonia told her isn't gospel, he imagines. But it ain't necessarily so, as the song says. Sometimes a customer comes into one of my shops, tries on a dress, and it looks terrific on her. But she might not realise it, because perhaps it's not her usual style, and she's used to looking at herself in a certain way. She needs to be persuaded that it really is "her".'

Nicole thought that Juana talked a lot of sense, despite her outspokenness, and she seemed to have a clear insight into her brother's personality. The trouble was, if she went along with Juana's reasoning, she had to accept more of the good side of Steve, to see the whole man, not just the black-painted villain of her young years. The more of this real person she admitted to her thoughts, the less easy it became to suppress the memory of his attraction for her. Only by insisting on his ruthlessness, his arrogance, his past duplicity, could she arm herself against his very real and potent charm.

He didn't come home the first weekend, so she had no chance to test the strength of her resistance, and Juana told her that he had phoned to say that he would be tied up in Madrid for several days. Juana's appreciation and censure of her brother were mixed in just about equal parts, Nicole had learned. Several times since she had been at Vistamar, Juana had been involved in long, low-voiced conversations over the telephone, from which she came away slightly tremulous and a little misty-eyed, leaving Nicole in no doubt that she had been talking to a man. And eventually she confided that this was so.

'Felipe—he's a consultant surgeon at the best hospital in Barcelona,' she said, with a dreamy smile. 'He's thirty-three, tall, dark, the sexiest eyes you ever saw, plays the guitar and drives a red Ferrari.'

'He sounds out of this world,' Nicole laughed. 'I should snap him up, if I were you.'

A dark cloud settled over Juana's normally lively face, dampening her smile and switching off the lights in her eyes.

'Steve doesn't care for him,' she said shortly. She stood up, brushing the crumbs from her full, floating aquamarine skirt. 'Must go—I have a business to run. I'm checking out some premises with a view to opening a boutique right here in Puerto de Castello. After all, those customers of yours will have to have somewhere to spend their *pesetas*.'

The jauntiness had reasserted itself in her voice, but not before Nicole caught the sadness and the mutiny in the amber eyes. Juana was in love, and well old enough to make her own choice, but for some reason, Steve did not like this Felipe of hers. And he had ultimate control over the purse-strings of her business. Had she, too, been faced with an ultimatum—give him up, or else?

Although she knew she might be treading on dangerous ground, she made a point of trying to do something for Lacey in what spare time she had. They swam and played tennis, and Nicole dragged her along, complaining, on walks in the hills, pointing out that exercise was very good for the figure. She also set out to help her learn Spanish better so she would feel less isolated.

'It will never work!' Juana said sceptically. 'Steve will demolish her in three sentences—you'll see.'

'If he does, I'll demolish *him!*' Nicole said grimly, the light of battle in her blue eyes. 'She's fourteen, Juana—can you remember how that felt? A woman and a child, locked in conflict under one skin! The moods, the doubts, the awful insecurity! And another thing—Lacey's not a loner by temperament.' As I was, she added inwardly. 'She needs friends of her own age.'

'How are you going to manage that, Señorita Fairy Godmother?' Juana challenged with a grin. 'Do you specialise in white rabbits out of hats?'

'Something like that,' Nicole agreed lightly. 'A family from London moved into one of the villas near the church yesterday, and they just happen to have a teenage daughter. I'm going to pay them a visit today, to check everything's all right, and I just might take Lacey along with me.'

'You're full of surprises,' Juana said. 'I wonder if my dear brother knows just how full—or if he's due for one himself!'

*   *   *

When Steve arrived home late on Friday afternoon, Nicole was the only one at Vistamar, apart from the servants. She'd had a hectic afternoon. One of her clients, an elderly lady, had fallen and sprained her ankle, requiring a visit from the doctor, and Nicole had needed to be on hand to soothe, assure and translate.

Hot and exhausted, she dropped her clothes in the linen basket from where Dolores, the maid, regularly collected them, then she put on her bikini, and did two slow-crawling lengths of the pool before stretching out flat on her stomach on the beige and green paving stones alongside. Although it was after five, the sun was still warm on her back, and she slipped the straps of her bikini top down her shoulders to avoid their leaving unsightly white lines across the even tan.

The warmth, the peace, and the blessed quietness, with only the soft ripple of the water and the light, playful breeze among the pines, did their work only too well. Nicole's eyes closed, and she began to drift off until she was on the borderline of sleep. Almost gone, she never heard the Mercedes glide smoothly up the drive. She was aware of nothing until a voice immediately above her said sternly, 'Don't you know how dangerous it can be to fall asleep sunbathing? If you had ever seen anyone suffering from sunstroke, you would know it was far from amusing.'

Steve!

The sound of his voice, the shock of his presence, jerked her back to instant reality, and she scrambled to a sitting position, forgetting the loosened straps of her swimsuit.

He still wore his lightweight business suit, but he had loosened the tie and removed the jacket, which he carried slung over one arm. The breeze ruffled his hair, and the contrast between casualness and formality carried a depth charge of sensuality, driving home to her with powerful, explosive force how strong was the pull of attraction which drew her to him. She wanted to grasp the lean, brown hands and draw him down to her, to run her own fingers through the dark hair in which the sun highlighted the streaks of russet, to touch the grooves at the side of that hard mouth, and watch it become tender with desire.

But that woudn't happen. He had told her very candidly what he thought of women who made use of their bodies' wiles to gain their ends, and she wasn't about to risk being raked again by his savage scorn. Besides, he was still a dangerous man, who was now also her employer, and she was not sure of anything about him, except that it would be madness to tempt fate by playing games with him.

'I wasn't actually sleeping,' she denied quickly, hoisting the bikini straps back into place.

'You weren't far off,' he said, and although he looked at her, there was nothing in his expression which told her he was in any way moved by the sight of her clad in two small strips of black nylon. His eyes paid her no compliments, revealed no admiration, and were no more concerned with her than they would have been had she been sitting by the pool in her grey pinstripe skirt and jacket. With a surge of bitterness, she realised that she had forfeited the right to his desire that night in his office. It had been there, briefly, but now his pride refused to let him think of her that way.

He glanced around, and changing the subject, demanded, 'Where's Lacey?'

'She's gone to the beach with the Astons,' she replied, and, seeing the instant question rise to his lips, added quickly, 'They're Sunstyle customers, a family from London with a daughter Lacey's age. The girls seem to get on well, and the Astons are nice people.'

'I would prefer to decide for myself who are "nice people" for my daughter to associate with,' he remarked, frowning.

'Oh, come on, Steve,' Nicole exclaimed with a short

laugh. 'How much choice do you have over her friends when she's in the States? Come to that, how much choice will you, or Sonia have over it for much longer? She *is* fourteen.'

Too late, she remembered his intention of dominating his sister's friendships, and half expected a battle. But to her surprise he shrugged and said, 'You're right, I suppose. I haven't had much practice at being a father, and it's not an inborn skill.'

He looked at his watch.

'I think I'll join you in the pool,' he said. 'Give me five minutes to change.'

Nicole was back in the water by the time he re-emerged, and she started to swim energetically, hiding from him, and from herself. He caught up with her quickly, reached the far end before her, and was waiting as she swam up.

No impulse in her life had ever been stronger than the one which made her itch to reach out her hand and touch the featherline of dark, damply curling chest hair.

'Not bad,' he said. 'Race you another length?'

The challenge in his eyes was too direct to be ignored. She might have killed his desire, but it was possible to re-earn his respect, and she could begin by meeting him squarely on any ground he chose. Including this one.

She put everything she had into that one, brief swim, inching back some of his lead with every stroke, and when she reached the other side, only a metre or two behind him, she was gasping and choking with exhaustion, holding on to the side of the pool with both hands as she struggled to regain her breath.

She felt his arms encircle her, supporting her in the water, and through her own blurred vision she saw a strange expression for once break the impassivity of his features . . . a look of mingled concern, incredulity and admiration.

'All right?' he asked, and she nodded speechlessly. 'I didn't intend for you to take it that seriously. I'll say this for you, Nicole—you're a fighter.'

Her hands automatically went up to his chest, feeling the wet, silken warmth of his skin beneath her palms. He did not let her go, neither did he pull her closer, but they remained transfixed in a small tableau, the water lapping gently around them, his eyes searching her face as she tried to conceal her excitement at his nearness, and the feel of him.

They were so absorbed that they did not hear the red Citroën race carelessly up the drive.

'Playing nicely, children?' Juana asked, looking down at them from the edge of the pool, a teasing, enigmatic smile twitching her mouth.

In a swift flash of instant reflexes, Steve released Nicole, hauled himself from the water, and made a grab for his sister's ankle. Realising his intention, she shrieked, jumped back, and fled across the terrace and into the house pursued as far as the french windows by her brother, shedding water everywhere.

He gave up the chase as she disappeared inside.

'Señora Alvarez will have my hide if I drip water all over her clean floors,' he said ruefully. 'I used to push Juana into the water, fully dressed, whenever she got uppity as a kid. She's getting uppity again.'

Uppity enough to want to choose her own lovers, Nicole reflected, reasoning that he knew full well getting her wet would not solve *that* one, and wondering exactly what he did intend to do. He'd have a plan, of that much she was sure.

'I think I'd better go change,' she said, towelling herself off briskly. She did not look at him. Her hands were still tingling with the tactile memory of how good it had felt to touch the wet, brown skin of his chest, to have his arms around her again.

It hadn't meant anything to him, she told herself soberly. He had merely been afraid that she was going to pass out in the pool. Not for the first time, she wondered how she would manage to live through the summer here. Between them, Vistamar and Steve were tearing her to emotional shreds, and when they had done, she feared she would be a drained and wrung out shadow of her former calm, contained self.

Briefly, she contemplated going to him and saying, 'Do what you wish, I don't care. I want out.' Then she thought of Lorraine, with her grey face and wasted body, dying at St Anthony's, supported by the thought of all that was left to justify her life—her daughter's success and happiness— and knew she could not take that escape route and go home in disgrace. See it through she must—and would.

Lacey, back from her excursion to the beach with the Astons, was already seated at the dinner table when Steve came into the dining-room and took his place. Nicole held her breath, waiting for the girl to greet her father easily and naturally in Spanish, as they had practised through the week until she had it perfect. But faced with her enigmatic parent, Lacey's nerve deserted her, and for a few moments she gaped at him blankly, while Nicole willed her to speak.

When she finally managed to dredge up somthing from her memory, she uttered the words with parrot-like woodenness.

'*El padre entra en la sala,*' she intoned expressionlessly. '*Está sentado en la silla.*'

Steve, surprised by this chanted commentary on his simple act of entering the room and siting on the chair, raised amused eyebrows.

'*Que niña tan intelligente!*' he observed, picking up his knife and fork to make a start on the tomato salad first course.

The sarcasm was only mild, and tempered with humour,

but Lacey was clearly stung by it. Jumping up from the table she blundered from the room, and they heard her footsteps running up the stairs to her bedroom.

'Has this household gone quite mad?' he enquired, aware that both women were glaring at him. Juana, who probably had expected something of this nature, shrugged resignedly, but Nicole could not restrain herself.

'She's been practising her Spanish all week!' she told him furiously. 'All right—I know it didn't quite work as it was intended to, but it woud have cost you nothing to be a little impressed. I dare say *you* can't remember how it felt to be young and insecure, and have some insensitive adult belittle your efforts. Come to think of it, you probably never *were* young and insecure!'

'Oh, boy!' Juana murmured, awestruck, lifting her wineglass to her lips. Nicole intercepted the amused horror in her eyes and, realising she had gone too far, waited for the bombshell of his wrath to fall about her head.

But Steve's reaction was unnaturally quiet, almost frighteningly so.

'As you so rightly point out, it *was* a long time ago,' he agreed. 'From the pinnacle of my advancing years, it is a little difficult to look back so far. But yes, I assure you, I *was* once young. Insecure? Does any of us ever stop being that?'

He stood up, pushing back his chair.

'I had better go and make my peace—properly, and in two languages,' he said drily.

They watched him go in astonished silence. After a while, in which neither of them touched their food, Juana said faintly, 'What have you *done* to him? I haven't heard him admit to anything as doubtful as insecurity in fifteen years!'

'Nothing. Not a thing,' Nicole answered, equally dazed by this sudden, unexpected glimpse of the vulnerability—the humanity—of Steve Rodriguez. 'He's probably coming down with something—the 'flu, perhaps. He'll be back to normal in no time. You see.'

But would *she*? Could she ever again look at life in simple terms of black and white, seeing him unequivocally as the villain of the piece, who had so much of her family's heartache to answer for? Whatever he had done in the past, he was not a monster, plain and simple. He was a man, with emotions of all shades, qualities both good and bad, hopes, ambitions, and, yes . . . fears, too. A man with whom she, heaven help her, was seriously in danger of falling in love.

CHAPTER EIGHT

TRUE to his word, Steve did not interfere unduly with Nicole's running of the agency. Having satisfied himself that she was in control of what she was doing, he left her to get on with it.

Both he and Juana were usually only home at weekends and, in between their visits, Nicole and Lacey settled into a fairly peaceable, routine existence. The girl seemed happier now she was making friends among the visiting holiday makers.

'It's about time that girl had some new clothes,' Juana said to Nicole, noting the general improvement in her niece's appearance. 'She and I should spend a few days in Barcelona, kitting her out and seeing the sights. I have to visit my shops there, anyhow.'

'And Felipe,' Nicole smiled, and saw the other woman's face cloud briefly before assuming its usual cheeriness. 'Juana? Nothing's wrong between you two, is there?'

'I don't know.' Juana bit her lower lip hard. 'Felipe is being rather odd lately. Evasive. He doesn't phone so often, and when I phone him, he makes some excuse to ring off after a couple of minutes. He *says* he still feels the same about me, but . . .' she hesitated '. . . I can't help wondering if Steve has been warning him off.'

Nicole shifted uneasily in her chair.

'Has Steve ever told you why he doesn't like Felipe?' she asked.

'He just says he isn't suitable for me, and then refuses to discuss it,' Juana said wretchedly. 'I know Steve virtually brought me up—I was still at school when our parents

117

died—but I'm twenty-seven, Nicole, and I've turned down proposals of marriage because none of them excited me as much as my work. Now, when I've finally met a man I really want, he seems determined to stand in my way. I can't understand it.'

Nicole felt for her in her obvious distress.

'But he can't really stop you, if you decide to go ahead and get married . . . can he?' she asked doubtfully, knowing all too well that Steve had ways of preventing anyone from crossing him. 'After all, it's not the Middle Ages.'

Juana frowned.

'You want to bet? He does, of course, retain ultimate control of my boutique chain, but I don't think he would use that against me. I'm still his sister, and besides, he'd have to look a long way to find anyone with my expertise. What worries me is that he might make things difficult for Felipe. He has all sorts of influence you would find hard to believe, stretching into many fields—like the tentacles of an octopus!'

Nicole didn't doubt it, and Juana's words brought back a recurrence of her old mistrust. Here was another innocent man, whose only crime was to love Steve's sister, about to be given the treatment. Nothing and no one was allowed to stand in his way, once he had made up that agile but implacable mind of his and decided they had to be eliminated.

The following day was Saturday, and Lacey had her heart set on going to a special teenage disco that was held at regular intervals in an old, converted farmhouse up in the hills. After a month in Spain, the Astons were due to leave for home on Monday, and this was to be the girls' final outing together. They had been planning it all week, and Lacey had anxiously awaited her father's permission when he arrived at Vistamar on Friday.

'It's all quite pukka and above-board,' Nicole assured

him. 'I've checked it out myself. It's properly supervised, only soft drinks are on sale, and the owner doesn't put up with any nonsense. Lots of Sunstyle's customers take their teenagers there.'

'Then I suppose I must trust your judgement,' he said. 'If the Aston girl's father will deliver them, I'll pick them up when it finishes. Your friend might as well sleep here tonight,' he told Lacey casually. 'There's no shortage of beds.'

Her expression of incredulous delight spoke volumes.

'Really? Then we can have tomorrow for swimming and things,' she cried happily. 'That would be great—thanks, Dad!'

She ran off excitedly to the telephone, and Steve raised his eyebrows laconically as he met Nicole's satisfied gaze.

'I think I've just been promoted,' he said drily. 'After two months of being "Father", I've suddenly acquired the status of "Dad".'

Perhaps you've started to behave like one, Nicole thought, wondering why there was this huge, ridiculous lump in her throat. But all she said, very lightly, was, 'Can't be bad, can it? But don't let success turn your head!'

'I think I've lost a little weight, but boy, there's still a way to go!' Lacey turned this way and that, surveying herself critically in the mirror before setting off for the disco. Juana had brought home an armful of baggy shirts for her to choose from, and she was wearing a brilliant pink one over her favourite jeans. 'Do you think any half-way decent-looking boy is going to notice *me?*'

'I have to tell you that not all boys like beanstick figures,' Nicole said. 'Take it from one who remembers—from experience. And you have the asset of a nice, clear skin. Lots of girls your age are spotty.'

'That's true. I don't have zits.' Lacey brightened a little, and abandoned her study of her reflection as she heard the toot of a car's horn outside. She clattered down the stairs in the canvas boots Nicole was sure were going to make her feet burn uncomfortably by the end of the evening, but which she insisted on wearing.

'I'm sure she doesn't really need all that stuff plastered around her eyes!' growled Steve, watching her departure from the windows of the *sala*.

'Relax—she'll be all right,' Juana laughed, but he was like a restless, caged circus beast all evening, prowling from terrace to *sala* and looking at the clock every half-hour. At eleven o'clock, his sister sighed in exasperation and announced that she was going to bed. The telephone, Nicole recalled, had not rung once for her all day.

'I said I'd pick them up at around eleven-thirty, so I'll be on my way,' Steve said. He glanced at Nicole, who was going through the motions of reading a book. 'Do you want to come for the drive?'

Crazily, her heart began to pound with fierce irregularity. Apart from that brief spell in the pool, they had never been alone together over the weeks she had lived at Vistamar. It had seemed to Nicole that he went out of his way to avoid situations where they might be, taking care that they simply did not arise. Now, quite unexpectedly, he had suggested she accompany him, a request she was at a loss to understand, but could not find it in herself to turn down.

'Why not?' she said casually, setting down her book. She was wearing only a skirt and a sleeveless top, but the July evening was very warm, so she did not bother to take a sweater. There was still an afterglow of light over the sea as they drove up into the hills, and away in the distance, the lighthouse at Cap Vol winked against the rocky, darkening coastline, echoed seconds later by its counterpart at Cap Faro.

'It's so beautiful,' Nicole said involuntarily. 'I hope it never changes.'

'All things change—even natural phenomena like mountains and beaches,' Steve observed. 'But they do it so gradually, and over so long a period of time, it's not noticeable. People can change too, Nicole.'

She turned her head sharply to look at his profile, wondering at his words.

'That I'm not so sure of,' she rejoined.

'Oh, no? Then you're still the same as you were at, say, Lacey's age?' he enquired probingly.

A shiver of apprehension crawled down Nicole's spine, and she wished she could steer the conversation well away from her past life.

'That's simply growing up. It isn't the same thing at all,' she said shortly.

'I don't agree. Even a mature adult isn't fixed immutably into a mould. The learning, changing process continues—it's harder and more painful, that's the only difference.'

'I think one thing we can be sure of, Steve, is that you and I aren't going to concur on too many subjects,' she said lightly.

'We could find plenty of areas of agreement if you weren't always hell-bent on resisting me,' he contradicted. 'Why do you do it, Nicole? Cast me as the villain, the bad guy, all along? I'm human, you know.'

The trouble was that she *did* know, or at least, was beginning to learn, and it was this gradual stripping away of layers of preconception which left her confused and uneasy. She was glad when the faint, distant sounds of music gave her both a distraction and a chance to change the subject.

'Listen,' she said. 'We're nearly there.'

Fortunately, he didn't pursue the matter, and minutes

later they drove up to the old farmhouse where the disco was being held.

The conversation had been skilfully carried out, so that from the outside the solid mass of the building looked much as it had when it was still a working farm. An enclosed courtyard and stables had been turned into a bar, and the music they had heard had drifted out from here, soft, smoochy ballads as a background to conversation, and for one or two couples who were dancing.

'Up here is stictly adults only,' Nicole said. 'The action is down in the basement, where it's well sound-proofed.'

He glanced at his watch.

'It's not quite half-past. Shall we have a drink and let them enjoy their last few minutes?' he suggested. Nicole did not demur.

It was pleasant to be seated out under the stars, sipping Martini and lemonade with Steve at her side. True, the conversation on the drive up had been a little fraught, and close to the bone, but he was relaxed and affable now, so much so that, in the atmosphere of friendly truce, she ventured to bring up something which had been troubling her mind.

'Steve, when you decided you wanted me to live at Vistamar, you said you didn't altogether trust me—you gave me the impression that you wanted to keep an eye on me,' she began. He did not deny or confirm this, merely spread out his hands in a gesture inviting her to continue, so, steeling her nerve, she did so.

'I've lived in your house for some time, now, and I think you'll admit that the agency is running efficiently, and there isn't any reason for you to have doubts about me, personally. You are only ever home at weekends, and then, any contact we have is minimal. So . . . what I want to know is . . . why is it still necessary for me to be there?'

'Aren't you worrying over nothing?' he asked lightly.

'As an arrangement, it works well enough. Your meals are cooked, your laundry is done, you can't deny that it's comfortable and convenient. If I do need to discuss business with you, it's easy for me to do so without having to search the village for you. Besides which, Lacey has been much happier since you moved in. I know it's your influence, and I *am* appreciative.'

Nicole was a little abashed by this unexpected gratitude. Praise from Steve was not handed out lavishly, and she never quite knew how to cope with it.

'I haven't done anything in particular,' she demurred.

'You've been there, you've talked to her, and listened, and sympathised. It helps that you're female, and a lot closer to fourteen than I am,' he said ruefully. 'I told you, I'm a very inexpert parent. Lacey was very small when Sonia and I split up. Naturally, the American court awarded custody to the mother, who was also American, so I only got to see her on occasions I was over there.'

'If I've helped a little, I'm glad,' said Nicole diffidently. 'It hasn't been any bother to me.'

'Everything's fine as it is, then,' he replied. 'So why rock the boat, Nicole? You get on well with my sister, don't you? I know she likes you. And right now, I feel she needs a friend.'

This was an opening Nicole simply could not resist.

'We all need friends, but Juana wouldn't be so miserable if you'd quit interfering in her love-life,' she said bluntly. 'She's twenty-seven, and has the right to choose the man she wants without feeling that *you* are trying to sabotage the relationship.'

He was deathly quiet for a moment and, in the stillness which suspended them, Nicole could hear her own heart beating. Once again, she had overstepped the mark, she knew from the closed expression on his face.

'Am I supposed to stand back and watch my sister make

a mistake that could ruin her life?' he asked curtly.

'But why should it?' she persisted.

'Nicole, this is really none of your business,' he told her, the affability gone, his voice stern and his eyes distant and withdrawn. 'I'm grateful for the way you have befriended my daughter and my sister, but don't try and push too far. This is a family matter, and I'll deal with it myself, without interference.'

Quivering with embarrassment, Nicole jumped to her feet.

'Exactly—it's not my business, nor did I want it to be, and that's why I don't want to remain at Vistamar!' she cried in a low, angry voice. The momentum of her own fierce emotions carried her out of the courtyard, through the arched entrance to where they had parked the car, and beyond. She was scrambling over rough, scrubby grass and stones, without quite knowing how she came to be there, stumbling in the darkness and scratching her legs on the thorny growth which impeded her.

He caught up with her swiftly, his hands on her shoulders arresting her, and turning her to face him roughly.

'You crazy female, you'll break your ankle, at the very least, blundering around out here in the dark!' he said scathingly. He still had a fierce grip on her shoulders, and she thought he was about to shake her as a terrier shakes a rat it has caught.

'Let me go, Steve, you hateful beast!' she spat at him, struggling. 'If I choose to break my ankle, or my neck, then that's my business! You've just told me to keep out of yours, so kindly do the same!'

'And let you injure yourself? Nicole, sometimes you are such a child!'

'Am I, indeed?' She stopped struggling, stung by this insult into action she would never have dared take in her right mind. 'A child, am I? Are you sure of that?'

Her hands slid up to his shoulders and then touched his face, inching their way along his jaw towards his ears, exploring his eyebrows and forehead, and finally crisping sensitive fingers through the thick springiness of his hair. Her body eased and curled itself into his, hips moulded to his thighs, breasts crushed against his chest, and, tightening her grasp in his hair, she drew his face towards hers, until at last his mouth touched hers.

The contact ran through them both like eager fire, scorching an unchecked path along their nerves, his tongue invading, probing, giving her no respite, his hands sliding down over her hips and pulling her more fiercely to him, so that she was left in no doubt of his arousal. She moaned and held him tightly, forgetting that they were only yards from the parked cars and the building full of people, wanting only to be taken and possessed beyond question.

He let her go almost as roughly as he had seized her, and she barely saved herself from falling.

'Oh, no, you don't!' he said contemptuously. 'That may be your favourite weapon whenever you need to score a point, or get your way, but you aren't going to use it on me again. If I *did* want to make love to you, it wouldn't be under those conditions.'

He ran a crisp hand through the hair she had ruffled, restoring its smoothness.

'Get back inside. It's time we picked up the girls.'

Nicole glared at him. What she had done was foolish and provocative, and she had only herself to blame for letting him rattle her so easily. And, once again, he had put her down. Once again, he had demonstrated that although, like any man, he could be temporarily inflamed, he could quite well resist her attractions. She wished fervently that she could be so blasé about his.

'I'll move out of Vistamar in the morning,' she announced coldly.

'If you do,' he relied in level, dispassionate tones, 'I think I should make it clear that I shan't be renewing your contract of employment. Do you really want to run home in disgrace?'

She turned her back on him and tried her best to maintain a dignified march back to the farmhouse, endeavouring not to stumble and make herself appear even more stupid. Whatever it cost her, she would not jeopardise her position now. Only two days earlier, she had spoken to her mother on the phone, assuring her that all was well, and then to Sister Cornelia, who had said that Lorraine was gradually loosening her grip on life, and she would send for Nicole as soon as she needed her.

'She's ready to let go peacefully now, and you are the chief reason for her acceptance of death,' the Sister had told her. 'She is content because your happiness and success are her vindication. The past . . . whatever it was . . . she has almost forgotten.'

Nicole would not be the one to disturb those old, unhappy memories. Some might say she was wrong to conceal the truth from her mother, but she would never be convinced of that. To spare her suffering had to be the greatest good, and, rather than risk her hearing a rumour of anything untoward, she would work for Steve Rodriguez, live in his house, and endure this unwilling, unreciprocated desire which made his presence a torment, and his absence an even greater one. There was no alternative.

Most of the drive home was mercifully filled by listening to the two girls chatter about their evening at the disco. Neither Steve nor Nicole had much chance to speak, had they wanted to, so their rather strained silence went unnoticed by the teenagers, who were totally absorbed by their own affairs. When they arrived back at Vistamar, Señora Alvarez made them both a drink of hot chocolate, and Nicole showed the guest to her room before turning in herself.

The last she saw of Steve, he was standing by the *sala* windows, gazing out across the terrace to the twinkling lights of Puerto de Castello, a glass of cognac in his hand.

'Night, Dad,' Lacey called breezily as they passed the open door on their way upstairs.

'Goodnight, girls. Sleep well,' he replied. Nicole wasn't sure if that benediction included her, but it failed singularly. She lay awake for hours recalling the burning touch of his lips and the hardness of his body, wishing, wishing, wishing . . . No sooner had she fallen asleep, it seemed, than the melodic plangency of the church bell reminded her that it was Sunday morning, and she had a family arriving at one of the villas today. Groaning, she turned over and buried her face in the pillow, wondering how she was going to struggle through the day.

By the time she had showered, dressed and forced herself to go down to breakfast, she had decided that it would be best endured by avoiding Steve as far as was possible. Since he and Juana were already seated on the sunny terrace, he reading a paper, it looked as if she would have to breakfast with him whether she liked it or not.

She made herself smile with what she hoped was at least normal politeness.

'No sign of the girls yet?'

'I doubt they'll surface before midday.' Juana yawned widely, as if she, too, had suffered a disturbed night. She looked at Nicole's crisp skirt and blouse, and ready handbag. 'Surely you aren't working today, are you?'

'I've just one family arriving. I thought I'd settle them in then drive down the coast to Ampurias and have a look at the Graeco-Roman ruins.'

Juana shuddered.

'You're welcome. History leaves me cold—I live for the

present,' she said. 'Haven't you seen Ampurias before, Nicole?'

Nicole hesistated.

'Long ago, when I was very young. I'll probably be more appreciative now,' she observed.

Juana's curiosity was aroused.

'Were you here with your family? You never talk about them,' she said.

Nicole very carefully spread strawberry conserve on her roll, avoiding Steve's eyes.

'There's only my mother and me. She's . . . she's in a hospice for the terminally ill,' she explained, reminding herself that this would mean nothing to him, that he knew nothing of what had happened to their lives after he put Teddy out of business and they went back to England.

'I'm so sorry.' Juana laid a slim, gold-braceleted hand on Nicole's arm. 'No wonder you don't speak of it. It must be painful for you,' she said softly.

'It's all right. I've come to terms with the inevitability of it, now, although I know it will still hit me hard when the end comes,' Nicole replied.

Still, she had not looked at Steve, and it was Juana who said, 'Our parents were killed in an air crash when I was still at school. It was awful—but it was a sudden, sharp shock, and at least they were together. It's bad for you to have to watch your mother die—it would have been dreadful for your father.'

'I don't remember my father,' Nicole said briefly, clinging to the knowledge that this was the literal truth. 'Excuse me—I must go, or my people will arrive before I'm there with the keys.'

She gathered up her handbag and car keys from the table.

'Drive carefully,' Steve said, before returning his attention to his paper. Apart from 'Good morning', those were the only words he had spoken to her. It may have appeared ill-mannered, but she could not bring herself to look back and acknowledge them.

Pounding the mosaic pavements of the ancient city complex under the broiling sun wore her out, and when she arrived back at Vistamar that evening, having stopped for a solitary meal in a wayside restaurant, she had a good excuse for going immediately up to bed. In the morning, both Steve and Juana were gone, and she was left to cope with Lacey, who was miserable because her friend had gone home. But she perked up as the week progressed, and on visits to the beach she saw some of the other young people she had met at the disco.

Now the season was in full swing, Nicole was kept frantically busy, and was glad she had scarcely a spare minute to think. At night, she dropped into bed exhausted, and first thing every morning was about her business. Somewhere in the back of her mind, she knew there was still her reluctant obsession with Steve, and as soon as she saw him again, whenever he sat by her side on the terrace, or his hand happened accidentally to brush hers, it would come flooding back with unassailable force. All she was doing was holding the tide at bay.

Still, she had not expected to see him until Friday, and her defences were unprepared when on Thursday evening, as she was drinking her after-dinner coffee on the terrace, the white Mercedes swept up the drive, with Juana in the passenger seat.

Nicole's hands gripped the edge of the table, and her heart felt as if it were first in her mouth, and then in her stomach. She watched him get out of the car, every line of his lithe body awakening a response deep within her, and then she saw that his face was etched taut with tiredness and responsibility. Juana was crying softly. She slammed the door as she got out, and ran upstairs without a word.

Steve pocketed the car keys, climbed the steps to the

terrace, and sank silently on to a chair. Nicole did not wait
for the housekeeper to appear. She fetched the cognac,
poured him a hefty measure, and left the decanter at his
side. He drained it, refilled the glass, and then she saw a
wry smile lighten his face.

'Did you have dinner?' she asked. It was neither very
original nor very elevated intellectually, but it was all she
could think of which might help in a crisis.

He shook his head.

'Food was not high on our list of priorities,' he said. 'But
I'm hungry now. Would you mind asking Señora Alvarez if
she could rustle up something?'

'All right,' she agreed. 'And then, you can call me an
interfering bitch if you want to, but I'm going to talk to
Juana—if she'll let me.'

To her surprise, he nodded. 'I think she will—and I think
you should. Is Lacey in?'

'Yes, but she's in her room, communing with Duran
Duran. I don't think she heard you arrive, and I shan't
disturb her!'

He stretched out on the cane recliner, briefly closing his
eyes, and Nicole knew a strong urge to smooth his forehead with her hands, not in desire, as she had on the night
of the disco, but to give him comfort. It was strange, this
notion that Steve Rodriguez might even need comfort from
her, and she stood for a moment, looking down at him and
trying to absorb its significance. Then the slate eyes opened
and regarded her steadily.

'Get on with it, then, or do I have to starve?' he asked
succinctly, and Nicole sped on her errand with a wry laugh.
That would teach her to be overcome by concern for him!

She could hear Juana sobbing quietly as she tapped on the
door of her bedroom. She did not answer when Nicole
called to her, but the door wasn't locked, and tentatively she
opened it, figuring that it certainly would have been had

Juana genuinely desired solitude.

Juana was lying flat on her back on her bed, her raised forearm shielding her face. Her shoes, bag and long cotton scarf were flung haphazardly on the floor, an indication of her distress in one so fastidious about her clothes and possessions.

'May I come in?' Nicole asked quietly.

Juana sniffed, blew her nose on a white, lace-trimmed hanky, and nodded bleakly.

'Do. You might as well be the first to hear what a fool I've been,' she said.

Nicole perched on the edge of the bed.

'It's Felipe, I take it?' she queried gently.

'Who else?' Juana forced a smile. 'He's married, Nicole. All these months, and I never knew. No wonder he never mentioned marriage in so many words! Apparently, he and his wife have been living apart for some years, but there's no question of a divorce.'

'Oh, Juana!' Nicole sympathised deeply with her distress. 'That's awful, but you mustn't think of yourself as being a fool. How were you supposed to know, if he hid it so well?'

'I should have guessed.' Juana was merciless with herself. 'There was always something not quite straightforward—reasons why I couldn't meet his family or close friends. Well, of course I couldn't—*they* knew! If I'd really used my head, I'd have come up with the right answers, but when you're in love, you see only what you want to see! Steve worked it out—he had some investigations set in motion, and they turned up this woman living in Zaragoza. I should have listened to him in the first instance, instead of being so stubborn, but I've been fighting Steve for so long, it's become second nature.'

Nicole smiled.

'I know what you mean. He takes that autocratic, no-questions-asked attitude, and you automatically find yourself at battle stations!'

'You, too?' A ghost of the jaunty grin flitted across Juana's mobile face. 'The craziest part of all this is that some hospital in Canada has offered Felipe a fabulous position. Isn't that just too convenient?'

Nicole did not miss the sarcasm threaded through her remark.

'One of Steve's connections?'

'Almost certainly, although he needn't have troubled. I've no desire to be a married man's "bit on the side", and I shan't see him again before he leaves. I'd rather stay a single career girl all my life, thanks very much!'

'Juana, you are far too attractive and intelligent to remain single unless it's from choice,' Nicole assured her. 'Is there anything I can get for you right now? I don't suppose you feel much like eating, but how about a drink, or some coffee?'

'Thank you, but no. I'd rather just spend the evening alone here, sorting myself out. But I'm glad I told you. It helps to talk to someone who doesn't think I'm a complete idiot!'

Downstairs on the terrace she found Steve finishing off the cutlet and salad the housekeeper had prepared for him.

'Coffee?' he invited, brandishing the pot. Nicole nodded and sat opposite him, regarding him somewhat warily, but he seemed to have recovered from his fatigue already, and she sensed no anger in him. 'How did you find her?'

'Not too bad, considering. A bit low, of course, and thoroughly annoyed with herself,' she told him. 'I think perhaps the worst is already over.' She raised her eyes to his, curious and slightly accusing. 'How long have you known?'

He seemed surprised by the question.

'Since yesterday, when my enquiries came up with the

wife's whereabouts. Do you think I regularly investigate every man who is interested in my sister?' he demanded. 'I just knew there was something about *him* that didn't ring true, and I don't see why she couldn't trust my judgement and take my word for it. But since she refused to do so, I decided to do a little research.'

'And to send him off to Canada, safely out of the way?' Nicole suggested, a touch of humour playing about her mouth.

'Ah, now, I haven't admitted to that,' he said, straight-faced. 'These medical eminences move around all the time, you know.' He refilled his coffee-cup, and suddenly stared at her with unnerving directness. 'Do you still think I shouldn't meddle in the lives of others?'

'In principle, yes.' Nicole was very cautious in her reply, because it was all too evident that there was meddling with the good of the individual at heart, and there was the other kind of interference, which had finished off her stepfather. It was difficult to lump them together. 'If you were going to find some dirt on Felipe, it would have been better to do so right away, rather than expect Juana to give up simply on your say-so.'

His eyes gave nothing away, but there was a stillness about him which put Nicole on her guard, convinced that whatever he was about to say, she would not find easy to answer.

'Shouldn't she trust me?' he challenged quietly. 'Wouldn't you trust a man whom you knew only wanted your good? A man who loved you?'

Out in the bay, a speedboat disturbed the silken sheen of the water, and from the pine forest behind them cicadas had begun to hum with the approach of night. But the sounds did not impinge on the absolute silence which held them enclosed in its spell, as Nicole struggled with her deepest self for an answer to a question which she knew was more profound than it appeared.

'Life has taught me that it's unwise to trust anyone blindly,' she said slowly, painfully. 'No one's motives are so pure they can't be questioned. I hope love wouldn't make me lose sight of that.'

'So young, and so untender,' Steve quoted, shaking his head with what she thought was amusement.

'So young, my lord, and true,' she quipped back, swiftly. 'If you want to be Shakespearean, I've played most of those heroines in drama club, except for Cleopatra.'

'Ah—but you aren't old and wily enough for the Serpent of the Nile,' he replied. Draining his coffee, he stood up, reaching deep into his pocket for his car keys. 'I'm off back to Figueras. See you tomorrow night.'

'You're going back—now?' Nicole said, surprised.

'I've an important meeting tomorow, and being the boss doesn't mean I can play truant whenever I feel like it,' he pointed out. 'When my staff are at their desks promptly at nine a.m., they can console themselves that the chairman is, too.'

'Oh, entirely laudable,' Nicole applauded. 'But wouldn't it be better to stay overnight and leave early in the morning?'

He paused, looking down at her, the keys jangling in his hand.

'Are you making me another of your offers?' he enquired lightly.

Nicole flushed, feeling the prickly redness run up her neck, hoping the gathering dusk would conceal it.

'Of course not! You're forgetting, all my offers have ulterior motives. Why should I make them otherwise?' she demanded with deliberate scorn, since the only weapon she still held was her own pride. He had her in his power, unable to leave either his house or his employment without consequences she dared not risk; he must not be allowed to think that she was eager to share his bed as well as his board.

'Obviously, there's no reason for me to hang around,' he observed. 'My presence isn't required by any of the women of my household. One is nursing a broken heart in solitude, another far too busy playing pop music, and the third——'

Pausing, he looked down at her, with that odd, searching gaze she found so disturbing.

'One day I'll figure out what the third wants from me,' he concluded, before getting into the Mercedes and driving off into the night.

CHAPTER NINE

NICOLE was just towelling herself off after an early-morning swim when she saw Juana's lone, slender figure approaching up the drive.

'I went for a long walk on the beach—all the way into the village and back,' she said. 'There's nothing like solitary walking to assist thought. I came to the conclusion that, although I'm miserable, and know I'm going to be miserable for some time, at least I don't have to worry and wonder about Felipe any more. I'm free of it all. And I can stop fighting Steve——' she grinned '—at least, on that issue.'

'That's great,' Nicole said encouragingly. 'You're well on the road to recovery, I'd say.'

Juana shot her a knowing glance.

'It won't be that easy,' she said. 'Have you ever been in love with anyone, and lost them? You haven't, have you? Somehow, you give the impression of being untouched and untouchable. Watch out—you'll fall all the harder when it does happen.'

'Perhaps I won't allow it to.'

'Perhaps you won't be able to prevent it,' Juana said percipiently, then changed the subject before Nicole could reply. 'I thought that this weekend I'd take Lacey on that shopping trip to Barcelona.'

'Good idea,' Nicole agreed. 'It would be a break for both of you.'

'I'll have to convince Steve I'm not intent on meeting Felipe on the sly,' Juana laughed. 'I should be well chaperoned, with a teenage niece along. We'll just do the shops, see a film, that kind of thing.'

Nicole thought it would be just the thing to give Lacey a
marvellous time, a weekend in Spain's second city with her
fashionable, youthful aunt. More than that, it would give
her an increased understanding of the Spanish side of her
personal heritage. There was still friction—she had been
torn in half for too long for the scars to heal miraculously,
but Nicole could see that things were easier between Lacey
and her father. Finding her using the computer one day, he
had been pleasantly surprised by her mathematical ability
and interest, and had promised to take her to his head office
to see the computer room there. It just might be, Nicole
thought, that father and daughter had more in common
than either of them had yet realised. She hoped that these
tentative roots would be strong enough to withstand the
rough edge of Sonia's propaganda treatment when she
finally reclaimed her daughter.

Juana, when she made up her mind, acted speedily.
Arriving home that evening, Nicole found a note addressed
to her saying simply, 'Gone to Barcelona—back Monday.'
She was glad for the pair of them, but the house felt
strangely empty, with only herself and the staff.

And then another thought struck her, with a blast of
apprehensive excitement. Steve!

'See you tomorrow night,' he had said, only yesterday.
tonight he would be home, and he and she, like it or not,
would have the place to themselves. She would be alone
with him, without the comforting neutrality of the presence
of others.

In the pit of her stomach, a fluttering sensation began,
and took over the rest of her body with invincible force.
Her legs were weak and trembly, her breasts ached, her
mouth was dry, and all because they were going to be alone
together.

Stop it! she told herself firmly. This was insane and

unreasonable. Was she afraid he was going to take advantage of the situation to make improper advances to her? The answer came promptly—no. He had plainly rebuffed her, had told her quite categorically that he thought her a tease and a user, and he wasn't interested in either.

What, then? What was it that was causing her to have such intense physical reactions? Nicole tried hard to find an excuse, but she could not avoid what was looking directly at her. It wasn't that she was fearful of what he might do, or nervous of her ability to defend herself. She wanted him to do all those things, to take her in his arms and kiss her, maddeningly and lingeringly, to touch her in all those intimate, sensitive places which tingled at the mere thought, and yes, to make love to her, to possess her, to silence this wild craving within her, once and for all. She knew that he wouldn't, that he neither needed nor wanted her as she was unable to stop wanting him, and it was this which was sending her quietly out of her mind.

And yet some natural female instinct to display herself at her best and most attractive made her come down to dinner dressed in a silky, royal blue dress which deepened the colour of her eyes, the cross-over bodice revealing tantalising glimpses of honey-tanned cleavage. A lost cause, she knew, but she couldn't help it.

Steve was late—he was usually here by this time—and Nicole, already in a fever of nervous anticipation, received a severe shock to her nervous system when she saw that the table was only laid for one.

'What about the *señor*?' she asked the housekeeper, surprised.

'He telephoned to say he will not be home tonight,' she explained, and the balmy evening disintegrated into bitter ashes for Nicole.

Why should he come home? Neither his daughter nor his

sister was here, and there was no reason why he should make the effort simply for her benefit. It was Friday night, and very likely he would be taking some woman out to dinner and the theatre . . . and back to his apartment afterwards?

Nicole picked at her food without interest. She had never known jealousy that was more than a mild pique before, and she had not realised that it could be a raging, gnawing pain that would not let her alone. She wanted to be with him—in every sense—and worse than that, she resented any woman who had what she could not. Was this what Juana had felt, when she learned Felipe was married? Was this what all the tragic heroines she had so glibly portrayed on stage experienced? Was it possible, then, that she was in love with him?

When you are in love, you see only what you want to see, Juana had said. But Nicole was not blind. Steve had not ceased to be who he was; in spite of all the admirable qualities she had come to recognise in him, that fatal flaw still existed. He remained the man who had ruined Teddy, who had once been capable of such unscrupulous action . . . and, it followed, might be capable of it still. And knowing this, she none the less desired him, was emotionally and physically enthralled by him, and a day, an hour, a lifetime, that was not in some way enhanced by his presence was less than worth while. If that was love, then she loved him, and loving him gave her nothing but guilt and pain.

He did not arrive home until late on Saturday night, and as he got out of the car Nicole observed that he was wearing a suit rather than casual clothes, and carrying his black leather briefcase.

'Goodness, you look as if you've come straight from the office,' she said lightly, trying to look nonchalant and unconcerned.

'I have,' he said shortly. 'But the office was in Geneva.'

'Oh . . . I didn't know you were out of the country,' she remarked. 'On Thursday you said you'd be home as usual, and I didn't realise there was a change of plans until Señora Alvarez told me.'

'As you know, things can come to a head suddenly, in business,' he said coolly. 'It isn't necessary for my housekeeper to know where I am, but since she's the pivot of the household, she needs to know if I am going to be absent. I can't think why *you* need to know, Nicole.'

He had not raised his voice above its normal, even pitch, but there was something so coldly insulting about his words that Nicole was as shocked as if he had drenched her in a bucket of iced water. For once, even the panacea of anger failed her, and she stared at him with wide, hurt eyes, bereft of response.

He didn't wait for a reply.

'I'm tired. I'm going to bed,' he announced briefly, and that was the last she saw of him until she came down, somewhat apprehensively, on Sunday morning, to find him already in the pool.

But his glacial, hurtful manner of the previous night might never have existed. He smiled at her as she slid into the water, the slow, unhurried smile that melted her bones and made her whole body ache with unsatisfied longings.

All she could do to relieve them was to let out some of the hurt she had been nursing through the night.

'I'm glad to see you're in a pleasanter mood, this morning,' she observed tartly. 'Last night you looked as if you had lost a shilling and found sixpence, as my old college tutor used to say—he never did catch on to decimalisation.'

Steve laughed.

'Last night you caught me on the raw,' he said. 'I'd had a hellish day, not improved by overlong delays at airports. I wasn't in the mood to be nagged. Anyone who lives here has to get used to my comings and goings.'

Nicole flushed beneath her tan.

'I wasn't nagging. I'm only one of your employees, and your comings and goings are none of my concern,' she disclaimed.

'You'll be telling me next that you missed me,' he grinned.

'Naturally, I missed you. The house was blissfully peaceful with you away,' she said, and taking a deep breath of air, dived underwater. The next thing she knew, he had grabbed her by the foot, and they both broke the surface, spluttering.

'That will teach you not to be cheeky to the boss,' he said amiably. 'Ah—breakfast has arrived, and I'm ready to murder it!'

The coffee was hot, the rolls fresh, and the sparkling morning promised to blossom into a scorching day.

'This afternoon, I *am* going to conform to the Spanish stereotype,' he said. 'I'm going to the *corrida* at Figueras. The bullfight.'

Nicole shuddered. Teddy had been a devotee of the ring, but he had never managed to persuade either his wife or his stepdaughter to overcome their reluctance and accompany him.

'Ugh—death in the afternoon, and all that!' she exclaimed distastefully.

'I see you've read your Hemingway,' he smiled sardonically at her across the table. 'But have you ever actually seen a fight?'

'No. I'm not a lover of bloodthirsty sports,' she said firmly.

He laughed gently, refusing to be provoked 'I'm far from being a regular spectator. But a friend of mine is fighting this afternoon, and he will be offended if I don't watch.'

Her eyes widened.

'Fishermen and matadors—what a varied lot your friends are!' she observed.

'I like it that way. Miguel and I have known each other since boyhood. Our fathers were friends, and we used to visit their ranch in Andalusia, where the bulls are bred. He's thirty-eight, now, and says this is his last season. The ring is a young man's business.'

'I wish your friend luck, and hope you have an enjoyable afternoon,' Nicole said.

'Do more than that. Share it with me,' he invited briefly, and she sat up straight, startled.

'Oh, no—I couldn't!'

'Why not?' he challenged. 'How can you condemn what you have not experienced?'

A chill of fear and fascination trembled along Nicole's bare arm. Blood and sand, violence and mastery . . . the soul of Spain was somehow interwoven with this bizarre spectacle, and sharing it with Steve would be more than simply an afternoon out. It would reinforce, subtly, the emotional bonds which spun her to him.

'That's not, strictly speaking, a logical argument, Steve,' she protested. 'I don't have to go over Niagara Falls in a barrel to know I wouldn't enjoy it.'

'I don't expect you to, Nicole,' he smiled, amused by the comparison. 'I'm only asking you to suspend judgement for a few hours, for something you should experience just once, if never again. Or are you afraid to?'

'I'm not afraid,' she said promptly, aware of having been manipulated, but unable to resist picking up the challenge. 'I'll go. But just don't be surprised if I faint, or throw up, will you?'

'Just let me know first whether I have to catch you or take evasive action,' he teased. 'Bring a sun hat, and something to protect your shoulders. Miguel has sent me two tickets for the *sombra*—the shade—where the best seats are, but it will still be hot.'

Nicole spent a lot of time deciding what to wear, and finally chose a halter-necked sundress teamed with a loose, unlined jacket.

'Aren't we setting off rather early?' she asked, as he ushered her into the white Mercedes.

'Not really. We're going to have some lunch, and I want you to meet someone who is rather special to me,' he replied mysteriously. He would not enlarge any more on the subject, and Nicole had to be satisfied with that as they drove up into the hills.

Her curiosity increased as he turned off down a road only just wide enough for the Mercedes to negotiate, which led, she knew from her own travels, to the tiny mountain village of San Martin de Castello. The little streets, scarcely more than pathways, were impassable for cars, so Steve parked the car just outside the village and they walked the short distance to the square, where the outdoor tables of two restaurants converged among the cool trees, and the shade of the houses around it. Above the village, the ruins of the old castle brooded over the pleasant scene. People were already enjoying drinks and *tapas*, and there was a mild buzz of conversation, punctuated by the twittering of birds seeking crumbs beneath the tables.

One tall old house fronted directly on to the square, and outside it, an old man was seated in a large armchair. He was portly, his face partly obscured by a grizzled grey beard, but his arms were sinewy, telling of someone who had once been strong and vital. His eyes were half closed, but they opened wide at the approach of Steve and Nicole, and the big hands clasped Steve's arm, drawing him down to a delighted but speechless embrace.

'It's good to see you, *Tío*,' Steve said, switching effortlessly into Spanish. 'I've brought someone to meet you. Her name is Nicole. Nicole—this is my uncle

Enrique.'

Nicole almost swayed on her feet, forcing down a gasp as here, in this sunny square, the past rose up again to haunt her. This old man was Enrique Rodriguez. who had once been Teddy's partner. She had met him occasionally, long ago, but he had changed out of recognition. She thought that he must have had some idea of how his nephew had treated his old friend, and yet here he was, grasping Steve's hand in obvious affection. Had he been in on it, too?

'Straight as a die, old Enrique,' Teddy had often insisted. 'I'd trust him with my life.' Nicole looked down into the eyes of Steve's uncle, and saw a smiling, almost childlike pleasure.

'Que linda, su esposa!' he grunted. 'She's so beautiful, your wife! But you will have to be strict with her.'

Nicole turned to Steve in bewilderment as a woman in a starched nurse's uniform emerged from the dim interior of the house.

'Oh . . . Señor Esteban,' she beamed respectfully. 'If I'd known you were going to call . . . only, your uncle is a little confused, right now. It's not one of his better days.'

'That's all right,' Steve assured her. 'We won't stay. It was only a passing visit.' He leaned over and embraced the old man. *'Adios, Tío.* I'll call again, soon, when you are feeling better.'

Taking Nicole's arm, he led her to a table outside one of the restaurants from where she watched, still puzzled, as the nurse led the old man into the house. She hardly dared ask what this was all about, but the questions must have been written clear across her face, and Steve did not keep her too long in suspense.

'He has Alzheimer's disease—more commonly known as senile dementia,' he informed her. 'It makes him very confused, and unable to remember events and place them in their proper order. Sometimes he has periods of remarkable clarity, at others, he's almost like a baby. Just now, he thought you were Sonia. He's forgotten all about the divorce, which took place all those years ago.'

'How very sad,' Nicole said, thinking of the wandering, helpless mind in the still healthy body. 'But I wish you had warned me.'

'He has days when he's almost as I remember him, when I was younger,' Steve said, his face expressionless, as it always was when he was in the grip of a strong emotion—why had she never realised that, until now? 'I keep hoping . . . although I know it's irreversible, as I suppose you do, with your mother. Although my uncle isn't going to die—he could live for years like that.'

'Which is just as tragic, in a way,' Nicole said. She could hardly meet his eyes across the table. Knowing that he, too, nursed a family grief, as she did, made her feel more closely bound to him than ever. Serves him right, she might have said, a few weeks earlier, but she could never again be so naïvely blinkered, so sure of right and wrong.

'As a boy, it was Uncle Enrique I admired,' Steve said, as the first course of mussels, anchovies and fish pâté arrived at their table. 'My father was a career diplomat, and rather a remote individual. But *Tío* Enrique was an entrepreneur, the founder of the family business. It was in his footsteps I wanted to follow. My father insisted I did it the educated way—university in England, then business studies at an American college. Maybe he was right. The day of the homespun, self-made man is almost gone. Modern business is more technological, more complex.'

'More Machiavellian?' Nicole suggested. She had not meant to say the words, but her own heart was clamouring desperately for different answers from the ones her mind already knew. Loving him, she wanted to believe in him, but stark, unalterable fact stood four-square in her path.

He gave her no answers.

'Perhaps,' was all he said. 'Anyhow, *Tío* refuses to move from this old village house he was born in, so we have the nurse to look after him. He's happy here—he can sit on his own doorstep and be right in the square, with life going on all around him.'

He looked up as the waiter arrived at their table.

'I challenge you to find better lobster anywhere in Spain,' he smiled, and Nicole had to agree that the fine crustaceans, lying on a bed of rice, surrounded by crisp salad, promised a superb meal.

'But not too much wine, or else I shall fall asleep during the *corrida,*' she laughed, thinking that perhaps it would be no bad thing if she did!

'No, you won't—not when Miguel is fighting,' he promised her.

Figueras was even more crowded than Nicole remembered it, and most of the traffic was headed in the direction of the Plaza de Toros. Outside, garish posters advertised the star performer, Miguel Delgado, and Steve hurried her in, assuring her that the *corrida* was one Spanish event which always started on time.

'Don't expect comfort, though,' he warned. 'Cheap or expensive, the seats are all hard.'

Nicole was relieved that theirs were in the shadier section. In the cheaper seats, which took the full force of the sun, she was sure anyone fair-skinned would grill alive. She observed the great, circular arena, larger than she had supposed from pictures she had seen, and imagined the loneliness of one man facing a dangerous beast across that vast, unfriendly expanse, with nowhere to hide. A thrill of horror and anticipation ran down her back as the blaring, pulsing pasodoble music heralded the parade of all the participants—picadors mounted on their beautiful horses, toreros, banderillos, and the three matadors, brazenly gorgeous in thier tight trousers and glittering jackets, the *traje de luces*, or suit of lights.

'Which one is your friend?' she whispered.

'The senior matador always walks on the right,' he told her. 'That's Miguel.'

When the ring was emptied of the procession, and the first bull was allowed to rush, snorting and pawing, into the ring, Nicole's heart began to pound, and she was tense with anxiety. It seemed an act of sheer insanity to put the slim, vulnerable person of Miguel Delgador in there with this fearsome creature.

'I knew I shouldn't have come,' she muttered.

'You can't leave now,' he said, smiling. 'Watch Miguel. He makes it look disgustingly simple, and he won't disappoint you.'

His hand found hers, and in its reassuring clasp her own clenched one slowly untensed, so that after a while she was able to forget her fear for the matador's safety, and admire the balletic grace with which he moved his body and the cape. She watched the picadors come on, and still had her hand in Steve's when Miguel returned to the ring for the *faena*, the climax, with his sword, and instead of the swirling cape, only the short, red *muleta*. She saw the bull manoeuvred so skilfully that he was planted head on in front of the matador. She saw Miguel balanced dangerously over the lowered horns in the breathless moment where, if he had judged it only slightly wrong, he would be tossed aloft, as helpless as a stuffed doll. Seconds later, she heard the swelling roar of triumph from the crowd, the stamping and cheering echoing round the arena. But she never saw the kill, for her head was turned against Steve's shirt, and her eyes were closed.

She was not ashamed of the instinct which left her unable, at the crucial moment, to come to terms with this violent and public death. But, aware of Steve's heart beating beneath her cheek, and his arms folded around her, she had known that she was where she wanted most to be, in all the world. It was blissful, ecstatic, but he had not chosen it, and when she finally drew herself free, she was puce with embarrassment.

'I'm sorry,' she said. 'That was idiotic of me.'

'It was no more than an automatic reflex,' he said tolerantly. 'You didn't hear me objecting, did you?'

She managed somehow to sit through the rest of the performance and tried to watch intelligently. For all her private reservations about this hangover from ancient Rome, it was impossible not to be affected by the emotion of the crowd and the occasion, the strange, mystical collective excitement all around her. When they left the arena, Nicole's knees were weak, and she was still gripping Steve's hand with fierce intensity.

'There you are—your first *corrida*,' he said teasingly.

'Probably my last, too,' she replied. 'It was quite an experience, but I don't think I could ever become an *aficionada*.'

'Maybe not. But it had you going a bit—admit it.'

'That's precisely why I shan't come again,' she said. 'I admire your friend's courage, but I still don't approve, and I don't want to be excited by something I disapprove of.'

From his quiet nod of the head, she saw he understood perfectly her mingled feelings of revulsion and fascination.

'Fair enough. But suppress your disapproval for long enough to meet Miguel.'

They shared *calamares*—delicious rings of squid, deep-fried in batter—and a carafe of wine with Miguel Delgado in a very plain restaurant tucked away in a back street.

'I come here because the food is good and, even more importantly, no one will expect to find me here,' he explained to Nicole, with a self-effacing smile. 'There are ladies who have very strange ideas about the romantic prowess of matadors, but I am a simple married man and father of three.

'That's the price of fame, *hombre,*' Steve grinned. 'Dodging the *corrida* groupies!'

Nicole found it difficult to reconcile this quiet, slight, modest individual with the elegant virtuoso who had earlier shown them what it meant to be alive, human, and walking the fine line between life and death.

'He isn't a bit as I thought he would be,' she said to Steve, as they drove back home through a golden evening, the mountains gentled by a diffused sunlight. 'I had this macho image in my mind, and then you introduced me to a nice, ordinary chap, with a wife and family! It's an enigma to me how someone so apparently normal can put his life at risk, over and over again.'

'Nothing is quite as it seems, Nicole,' Steve said gravely. 'All of life is a puzzle, which you can look at from many angles, seeing a different picture—but never the whole. Everyone is like that, too. Miguel, you, I, the people you see in the streets. There is never just one dimension.'

She did not answer. Today, she had encountered yet another dimension of him, involved in and understanding a spectacle that was inherently Spanish. She had seen again how tolerant and thoughtful he could be, and perhaps for the first time, in these unlikely circumstances, she had been at ease in his company.

But as he brought the Mercedes to a halt in the drive of Vistamar, he turned to her, and rested a hand lightly on her bare shoulder, his fingers moving exploratively over her collarbone, and she quivered. The raw emotions aroused by this afternoon of violence and excitement had left all her senses exposed, so that she was incapable of hiding how deeply his touch thrilled her. Without a word he got out of the car, opened the door at her side, and held out his hand,

and without a word she took it, and walked with him into
the house.

All was silent—he had told the staff that they would not
be needed for the rest of the day—and in the silence, Nicole
could hear the deep, steady beat of her own heart as they
stood together in the hall. Slowly, his hands on her
shoulders drew her closer to him and, as if it had been pre-
ordained, his mouth found hers, biting gently and then
more demandingly at her lips until they opened to him, like
a flower, and the sap of desire began to flow through both of
them in equal measure. His fingers unpinned her hair and
threaded themselves through it until it fell in a loose, untidy
cascade of sensual dishevelment around her face.

'I'm tired of playing games with you, Nicole,' he said
softly. 'The skirmishing is over, and it's time for the
moment of truth.'

She nodded speechlessly, unable to control the drumming
of blood in her ears, and the almost unbearable impatience.
She had been ready for this moment for so long—longer,
perhaps, than she even knew herself—and now, she went
forward to meet it with an unfeigned willingness, and no
coy pretence of reluctance.

She never knew how her legs allowed her to reach her
bedroom, only that his arm was firm around her waist, but
finally the door was closed behind them, and the last of the
sunset streaming through the windows caused her no
shame. She wanted to see him and be seen by him, to know
this experience second by second, inch by inch, and she felt
no shyness as he deftly untied the halter straps of her dress
and let it fall to the ground.

He drew the shirt over his head, and pulled her to him; as
their bodies touched, she exhaled a long sigh of delight, her
hands moving slowly up his back, savouring the raw silk
texture of his skin. As one, they sank on to the waiting bed,
his hands cradling her breasts, his mouth teasing their tight

peaks until she cried out aloud for mercy.

He gave her none. The rest of their clothes were swiftly discarded, and then there was nothing but his taut, hard body moving against hers, bringing her to fever point and then tormentingly letting her go, to start all over again, until she was ready to die of anticipation and longing. She heard herself moaning, begging, uttering meaningless words and cries she could not hold back, arching herself towards him and holding him to her, her nails digging deep into the strong muscles of his shoulders.

With a low laugh of male triumph, at last, sensing her readiness, he eased inside her, and so carefully and expertly had he prepared her for this moment that the split-second of pain was swallowed up in the immensity of pleasure; she could not have said where one ended and the other began. They moved together in a symphonic unison of sensation where nothing jarred or grated, but, like music, took them ever and inexorably onward, flowing, merging, until they reached together the final, blissful notes of conclusion.

Nicole lay at peace on the far shore of this astounding and revelational experience. She had wanted him, and fought that need almost from the beginning, and there had been a time when she thought desire was only a craving to be satisfied. But she knew, now, that this was not the whole of it. Making love was not a gift you gave to another, or took from them, but a union in which the giving flowed back and forth. He had given in abundant measure, as much as he had taken—and so had she. And what she felt for him was not, now, at an end, but only at the beginning, stretching ahead further than she could hope to see.

In the warm aftermath of loving, she had not yet begun to question what had happened to her, how she had allowed herself to form so passionate an attachment to a man she had started out hating, and just where she imagined this relationship would lead her. It was enough to drift off to sleep curled against him, as sensually content as a well-stroked cat.

She awoke in the night hungry for him once more, finding him ready for her, and they came together with increased passion in the moonlight-silvered room.

'I never knew it could be like this,' was what fictional heroines often claimed, but somewhere in the deep, inarticulate core of her being, Nicole had known exactly, from the moment he had come back into her life . . . that if and when they made love it would be unforgettable and inimitable. Other men would be no more than pale shadows of Steve Rodriguez, who, in her heart and mind, had been her lover long before he had ever touched her, and always would be, even if he never touched her again.

She awoke in the early morning to faint sounds of someone moving, and, stretching out her hand into the emptiness where his body had been, knew he had left her bed. Opening her eyes, she saw him pulling on his shirt.

'Good morning,' he said politely, as if they had not spent a gloriously abandoned night giving each other every imaginable pleasure, but had just met on the street. 'I didn't mean to wake you, but I figured it might shock Dolores when she brings your early-morning coffee to find me here.'

Nicole stretched, the sheet falling away from her slender nakedness.

'Sneaking away without saying a word, were you?' she asked lightly. Just to see him standing here, fastening his trouser belt around his waist, and regarding her quizzically, made her stomach muscles tighten involuntarily. 'Do you have to go already?'

She was smiling, still warm and happy with the memory of what had been, for her, a profound and magical experience, so it came as a shock to see his forehead contract into the familiar frown which hardened his face.

'Nicole, I am not a performing seal,' he said testily. 'I

might remind you, in case you had forgotten, that it's Monday morning, and the working world hasn't gone away.'

Rebuffed, she drew the sheet up to her chin and stared at him, puzzled. 'I know that, Steve. I didn't expect that you and I were going to spend the entire day in bed together.'

'You surprise me,' he said drily. 'I've known women half your age again, and vastly more experienced, without half your . . . capacity for passion. Last night was a revelation, Nicole.'

It came across as more of a criticism than a compliment, and Nicole felt a red tide of shame rising within her. To her, the night they had just spent together had been little short of a miracle . . . she had thought it was the same for him. He had certainly behaved as though it were. But then, to her it was all new; perhaps, to him, she was just another woman, and experience made passion an easy matter to simulate. He looked so stern, so hostile, now, that she knew a fierce urge to cry. She wanted to throw herself into his arms and beg him not to be so cold, when only hours before he had been so loving. But she refused to lower herself that far.

'I'm sorry,' she said stiffly. 'As I suppose you realised, I'm a novice at this game. I'll bear it in mind . . . in future liaisons . . . always avoid showing enthusiasm.'

He shook his head in mild exasperation.

'Forget I said it. I didn't intend to conduct a post-mortem,' he said. 'I have to go, now. I still have to shave and shower, and I want to be in Figueras by nine.'

Bleakly, she watched him leave the room. You botched it, Nicole, she told herself wretchedly. He expected a shy virgin he would have to coax and persuade a little, and you fell into his arms with all the reluctance of a ripe plum! But what should you do, when your first experience of making love came with a man you wanted with an all-devouring, obsessive passion?

All hope of going back to sleep had fled now, so Nicole got out of bed, went into her en suite shower, and turned the water on full, soaping and scrubbing with something like distaste the body she had given him so willingly, treating it as though it were an instrument of betrayal rather than one of pleasure. Without too much thought she pulled on a skirt and top, pushed her feet into sandals, and went down to breakfast. She had thought of waiting until he had left, but that was the coward's way out, and she would not let herself take it.

He was seated at the terrace table, crisply suited and distantly businesslike, white cuffs just showing below his sleeves, grey silk tie knotted at his throat. She had not intended to refer to what had happened between them, but a great swell of resentment and unhappiness overwhelmed her, making it impossible not to speak her thoughts.

'Business as usual then, is it?' she asked, unable to prevent bitterness creeping into her voice. 'Last night was just a one-off, an aberration?'

He looked up from the papers at the side of his plate, which had been receiving more of his attention than she had.

'Men and women do go to bed together, Nicole,' he said evenly. 'Then they get up and go about their everyday affairs. It's called life.'

'Very funny, Steve. You're a master of sarcasm,' she snapped back. 'Thanks a lot for using me!'

She had his attention now, full and undivided, but the unpleasant gleam in his eyes and the tightness of his lips sent a shiver of fear along her nerves.

'It's a question of who used whom, isn't it?' he demanded. 'But then, that's the way it's been all along in this relationship, hasn't it—*young Nicky?*'

All the blood, all the liquid sap of life seemed to run

from Nicole's body, leaving her dry and dessicated, a paper figure that the breeze from the pines might blow away. Only her mother and Teddy had ever called her that, years ago, when she was not much more than a child. It was a pet name from the past, which had nothing to do with Nicole Bradbury, and gazing mesmerised into the hard, challenging slate-grey eyes of the man across the table, the man who had taken over her life, her heart, and now her body, too, Nicole saw the truth with dreadful certainty, and saw what a naïve fool she had been to take on such a consummately clever opponent. He knew, and must have known all along, exactly who she was. So what game had they been playing, all summer?

Whatever it was, Nicole realised bleakly that she was the loser.

CHAPTER TEN

'BUT of course I knew you were Teddy Walton's step-daughter,' he said, stirring his coffee and regarding her with that half-smile he reserved for those he considered incompetent idiots. 'Didn't I tell you I make it my business to know all there is to know about anyone moving in on my patch?'

Nicole was still too shocked to speak coherently.

'But . . . how . . . I don't understand,' she said lamely. He shrugged.

'It's not difficult to unearth information about people, with the resources of a large organisation at one's fingertips. And it's essential to have that information, since it may prove relevant. Your mistake, Nicole, was in trying to take me for a fool, assuming you could hide from me anything you didn't want me to know.'

The blood had begun to flow through her veins again, reviving her instinct to fight. She had come to Spain believing him to be her enemy, and could do so again, if that was the way he wanted it.

'Was it necessary for you to know? In your own words, was it relevant?'

'Maybe not. How was I to know? But the fact that you chose to hide it was deeply significant. It made me wonder what you were up to. It made me distrust you. I gave you every chance to tell me, but you deliberately persisted in keeping your supposed secret.'

She winced at his scorn, remembering clearly now all those hints, the remarks and asides which she had taken to be unfortunate coincidence.

'You could simply have told me that you knew,' she said. 'Or wasn't that sufficiently devious for you?'

'I wouldn't have got you to reveal your hand by showing my own, would I?' he replied. 'Besides, why should I have told you? I wasn't hiding anything from you. You knew exactly who I was.'

At last, at last she could voice the accusation that she had suppressed ever since she knew their paths would cross!

'Yes, I know who you are,' she said with cold satisfaction. 'You're the man who ruined my stepfather and cheated him out of his share of the business. You're the man who turned us out of our home and sent us back to England with nothing. You're right—I've been incredibly foolish. How *could* I have begun to respect and trust you? How *could* I have sunk so low as to let you ... to let you ...'

She couldn't finish, but he was looking at her enquiringly, his brow clear, without even the grace to react with a little shame to her accusation.

'To let me make love to you?' he supplied smoothly. 'As I recall, I didn't have to work too hard to get you into bed.'

Nicole shuddered fiercely with humiliation and distaste.

'God, I hate you, Steve Rodriguez!' she exclaimed fervently. 'I should have followed my first instincts where you were concerned! My mother warned me to keep out of your way, and she was right! Once a snake, always a snake! How could I forget?'

He didn't move, not so much as a muscle twitched in the lean face, and his hands lay perfectly reposed on the table, with no uneasy fidgeting disturbing the strong fingers.

'You've waited a long time to throw that in my face, haven't you?' he suggested. 'I wonder if you feel any better, now that it's finally off your chest? I did wonder, in view of your secrecy, whether you had come to Spain with some sort of twisted desire for vengeance in your mind. And then I wondered whether your plotting might be against my person, rather than my business, to get me involved with you, sexually and emotionally, and then ditch me.'

Inside the house, Nicole was vaguely aware that the telephone was ringing persistently. Its shrilling tone jangled her already shredded nerves, and she curled her fingers into her palms, feeling the bite of her own nails.

'If you think that I'd descend to that kind of manipulation——' she began furiously, and then a light footfall distracted them. It was the young maid, Dolores, who stood with the portable telephone in her hand, looking from one to the other of them, aware, as she could scarely fail to be, that an argument was raging, and fearful to interrupt.

'*Por favor* . . . there is a call for Señorita Bradbury,' she whispered uncertainly. 'It is from Inglaterra, and the lady says it is most urgent.'

'Thank you, Dolores.' Nicole took the telephone from the girl, who scuttled off back into the house, away from the battle area, and a moment later she heard Sister Cornelia's voice, calm, practical but insistent.

'My dear, I think you had better come home right away,' she said. 'The time is very near—she can't last much longer, and she is asking for you. Can you do that?'

On the warm, sunny terrace, Nicole was suddenly chilled clean to the marrow of her bones.

'Yes,' she said unhesitatingly. 'Of course, Sister. I'm on my way.'

She had given her answer unequivocally. Lorraine was dying, and the only thing that mattered now was to be at her side, but as she lowered the phone to the table, and the reality of the news hit her, shock siezed her, a panicky indecision paralysed her thinking and immobilised her limbs.

Through this nightmare fog, Steve's level, authoritative voice cut a single clear pathway.

'What is it?' he demanded. 'Nicole—pull yourself

together and tell me what's happened.'

She stared at him, still too shocked to react properly.

'It's my mother. Sister Cornelia says the end is near—I have to go to her!' she muttered. Thinking aloud, she continued worriedly, 'But it's the height of the season—will I even be able to get a flight?'

Steve stood up.

'Leave that to me,' he said firmly. 'Go upstairs and pack what essentials you need. Now, Nicole.'

He came round the table and turned her inert form in the direction of the house, giving her shoulders a little shake to get her moving. His touch galvanised her, and, responding to his decisiveness, she sped upstairs to her room and began to fling things haphazardly into her flight bag, stuffing her passport and money into her handbag with hurried abandon. By the time she came down again, the Mercedes was ready, with the engine running.

'All arranged,' he said briefly. 'Hop in—we have to make Gerona in record time.'

It seemed only minutes earlier that they had been locked in a bitter dispute, accusation and counter-accusation hurled across the table at one another. Now, belted tightly into her seat, Nicole sat with her hands clenched in her lap as he negotiated the hairpin mountain roads at a speed she would not have believed possible. They reached the airport with time to spare, and, in her zombie-like state, Nicole did not ask him why when he collected not one ticket but two, and hustled her swiftly into the departure area. She was only too glad to give her entire energy to reaching the hospice in time to be with her mother when the end came. She never questioned Steve's presence at her side, and for the present, this morning's awful discovery and all that had followed from it were blotted from her mind. In fact, she said scarcely a word to him, nor did he trouble her with conversation, either. Her vision was narrowed down, limited to what lay immediately ahead, and must be borne, however sad and harrowing she knew it would be.

But in the recesses of her disturbed consciousness she was aware of him, ushering her off the plane and swiftly through Customs with the ease of one accustomed to and untroubled by officialdom, helping her into the already waiting hire car and driving off with only a minimal request for directions. It wasn't that she was not too proud to lean on his strength, his powers of organisation, his rocklike steadiness. At this crisis point in her life she was, quite simply, incapable of functioning independently.

The day was sunny, but there was a cool, stiff breeze, and it was Steve who reminded her to take a sweater from her flight bag, since they had left the Spanish heat far behind them. He draped it around her shoulders as they got out of the car in the grounds of the hospice.

'At St Anthony's, we don't make dying a gloomy business,' Sister Cornelia had promised Nicole when Lorraine was first admitted. Now, she welcomed her with a smile, as if she had just dropped in for a visit, and remarked on how speedily she had got here, before turning her mild, enquiring gaze to Steve.

'My . . . employer, Mr Rodriguez,' Nicole said faintly. 'Is there somewhere he could wait?'

'Surely. But he can come and have a cup of tea in my office, first of all.' Sister Cornelia took Steve's arm. 'Go along, dear. You know the way. I'll be along in a while.'

Everything was so blessedly calm and normal that Nicole's frantic pulse-rate began to steady a little. She looked at Steve, really seeing him for the first time in hours, and a slow, reassuring smile creased his mouth. She knew a brief, irrational desire to have him with her, lending her his firm assurance and sharing with her this deeply painful ordeal, and involuntarily, her hand went out towards him.

He shook his head, pressing her fingers lightly with his and letting them go again.

'You know I can't come with you,' he said, and she thought she detected the faintest echo of regret in his voice. 'But I'll be here as long as you need me.'

The look that passed between them said it all without words. She had fought him with every weapon in her arsenal, and only grudgingly had given him the respect he exacted; she had stumbled hesitantly towards understanding, and surrendered to him with a passion which broke all barriers . . . except this final one, the unacceptable shadow of the past. He was yesterday's enemy, and she could not escape from yesterday. It ended here, and she knew that he, too, acknowledged that truth.

Lorraine's room was bright with flowers and sunshine. She was heavily sedated, but conscious, and her weak smile left no doubt that she recognised her daughter.

'Nicky,' was all she said, and Nicole took the wasted hand between her two young, strong ones as she sat by the bed. They did not talk—Lorraine was already beyond the point where rational conversation was possible, but the warm communion of love flowed palpably between them, and the hours ceased to register for Nicole, sitting there, holding the hand which had so often held hers as a child, profoundly glad that she had been in time to go with her mother a little way along this untrodden and unknown road.

Some time later, Lorraine began to mutter a little, drifting in and out of semi-consciousness. Nicole knew that her mind had wandered back in time as she rambled half coherently about her own youth, speaking the name of her first husband, the father Nicole could not remember. And then she stiffened slightly as her mother seemed to imagine that she was back in Spain again, with Teddy.

Her head moved restlessly on the pillow.

'No . . . Teddy . . . can't give up Vistamar . . .' she mumbled. 'Our home . . . poor Nicky, it's not fair! You have to fight him, Teddy . . . have to fight that devil Rodriguez, don't let him . . . do this to us . . .'

Her distress was all too real, even in this drugged, comatose state, and Nicole reached for the bell to ring for Sister Cornelia. But, with well-timed prescience, Sister arrived, accompanied by a nurse who gave Lorraine an injection, and very soon she was peaceful again.

'She didn't know what she was saying, you know,' Sister Cornelia said placatingly, noting Nicole's white, strained face. But Nicole was not comforted because, if only on a subconscious level, she knew, Lorraine had meant every word. She spoke no more after that, but sank deeper and deeper into unconsciousness. The slow summer dusk was beginning to close in as Lorraine sighed, took a deep breath, and then was still. As easily and painlessly as that, it was over, the moment Nicole had dreaded and waited for. Her mother had peace at last, but she, now, was truly alone.

Steve was waiting in the corridor when Sister Cornelia gently persuaded Nicole to leave the chair she had occupied for so many hours, and led her from the room.

'Take her home now, Mr Rodriguez,' she said quietly. 'It's over. The formalities can wait until tomorrow.'

Nicole walked slowly out into the car park, Steve at her side, close to her but not touching. He opened the car door for her and she stood for a moment before getting in.

'Please would you give me a lift back to my flat?' she asked politely, distantly. 'I'm grateful to you for getting me here, and . . . everything, but I can manage on my own, from now.'

'Like hell you can!' he retorted, pushing her shoulders and easing her into the seat. Slipping into the driver's seat, he started the engine. 'I know your opinion of me, but it would take a baser character even than mine to turn you loose alone tonight!

She was not capable of argument, and sat woodenly, drained of all feeling, as he drove back to London. That night she slept alone in the tasteful luxury of the hotel suite Steve kept in London, in blessed oblivion, courtesy of the doctor he summoned who gave her a sedative to make her sleep.

Lorraine's funeral took place two days later, on a beautiful summer morning with the trees around the small church near the hospice in full leaf, and alive with careless birdsong. Apart from Sister Cornelia and several other members of staff, Nicole and Steve were the only mourners.

She had spent the intervening days in the hotel suite, from where he had accompanied her to make the funeral arrangements, shop for a suitable black dress, and attend to all the complications death involves the bereaved in, at a time when they are least able to cope with it. Meals had been sent up from the dining-room, and he had spent some time quietly conducting business over the phone. Apart from what was essential, they had talked to each other very little.

But he had been *there*, calm and indisputably in control, easing her through the formalities and ensuring that nothing troubled her more than it absolutely had to. She knew that he had rescheduled all his appointments for the week, and acknowledged that, without the solid bulwark of his presence, these days would have been far more difficult to endure. For that, it was impossible not to feel gratitude.

On the second night at the hotel, she had awoken from a brief sleep with every nerve and cell raw with pain, the merciful anaesthetic of shock having finally worn off. Alone and grief-stricken in the darkness, she had longed to slip from her bed and run to Steve's room, to bury herself in his arms and find assuagement in the unfailing physical passion he aroused in her. She muffled her face in the pillow and shed the first tears since she had walked from St Antony's.

Her mother was dead, and she was in love with a man she could no longer allow herself to love. Nicole sobbed silently and helplessly until at last, worn out, she dropped back into an exhausted sleep.

The morning of the funeral she awoke early, pulled on her wrap and went into the suite's comfortable sitting-room. Switching on the kettle to make tea, she drew the heavy curtains slightly and gazed down at the panorama of half-sleeping streets and leafy parks far below.

The door opened softly, and turning, she saw Steve, in pyjamas and a maroon velour dressing-gown, running a hand through thick, sleep-ruffled dark hair.

'I thought I heard the kettle boiling,' he said. He pulled the curtains wider, letting the early light flood into the room. 'This is the best part of the day in London, or any city. In Puerto de Castello the fishing-boats will have just gone out, and the sea will be like blue silk.'

Nicole made tea in two of the fine china cups. Mention of Puerto de Castello disturbed her; it transported her back, briefly, to a lost golden world of sunlight and warmth, where for a short space of time she had been a gullible idiot and deceived herself into believing she could love this man. It had been an illusion. He had never really cared for her at all, even when he was making love to her. As he had destroyed Teddy, so he had laid waste her life, too . . . only the method differed.

But . . . something lingered persistently, a nagging memory of the Steve she had begun to learn to know and appreciate. It would not quite lie down and die, and, if only for the way he had stood by her through these terrible days, when he had been under no compulsion to do so, Nicole felt that she owed him at least his day in court.

'Steve,' she began hesitantly, 'if I ask you something, will you answer me—truthfully, to the best of your ability?'

He looked thoughtfully at her before replying.

'Fire away,' he said lightly.

She took a deep, steadying breath.

'Will you tell me . . . or rather, give me your version of what happened in that business between you and my stepfather, ten years ago?'

His gaze did not falter, nor could she discern anything significant from it.

'What should I tell you? You already know it all, don't you?' he asked brutally. 'Your mother has told you, and I don't doubt Teddy had plenty to say. There's nothing that I can add. Let it go, Nicole.'

He turned his back on her to stare out of the window, broodingly silent, and Nicole accepted the *coup de grâce* he had given her hopes. She had wanted to believe in him, wanted him to tell her of some mitigating factor which would reveal him as, if not exactly innocent, at least not wholly culpable. She had prayed for a grey area to explain the inexplicable, but he had admitted from his own lips that there was none. So, on the same day that she buried her mother, Nicole said goodbye to love.

When they were alone in the churchyard after Sister Cornelia and the others had left, Nicole turned to Steve, austere in his dark suit beside her, and drove the knife into her own heart.

'You know that I can't come back to Spain, don't you?' she said. 'I can't work for you any more, not now.'

He didn't answer, just looked at her with his unreadable grey eyes unusually dark, and she hurried on.

'I know I'm breaking my contract, and if you want to penalise me for that, or dig up those trespass charges, or make it impossible for me to get another job—well, so be it. It doesn't matter any more now, because now that my mother is dead, she can't be hurt by anything that happens to me.'

'So that's why you forced yourself to work for me all

summer, why you made yourself live in my house—the one
you believe is rightfully yours—and endured the company
of my daughter, and my sister,' he said, the old, hard scorn
creeping back into his voice. 'To say nothing of trying to
persuade me that you found me fatally attractive. You went
a little over the top, there, didn't you?'

He dug his hand deep into the pocket of his suit and drew
out the keys of the Mercedes.

'You can phone for a taxi from here, I presume?' he asked
coldly. 'Pick up your stuff from the hotel any time you
like—I shan't be there. If you really, honestly believe I
would do any of those things you have just suggested, if,
after all this time, you still don't know me better than
that—well, I don't think I want to be in your company a
minute longer. Goodbye, Nicole.'

The following weeks passed in something of a daze for
Nicole. She had no further personal contact with Steve, and
expected none, but all her clothes and possessions arrived at
her flat, sent on from Vistamar, as if to prove conclusively
that not only had he taken her seriously, but himself no
longer wanted anything to do with her. Not long
afterwards, a neatly typed testimonial affirming Miss
Nicole Bradbury's competent and industrious attitude
towards her work, and her soundness of character, signed
simply 'Esteban Rodriguez' slipped through her letterbox.
He had placed no obstacle in the way of her finding another
job, and she was free to pursue her career as she chose.

'But why, Nicole?' asked Peter Delamere, when he
phoned her to offer his condolences on her mother's death,
and to discover what had caused her to leave Sunstyle. 'I
know any of our rivals would snap you up, with your
abilities and experience, but *why* was it necessary for you to
leave? You had it all going for you—a great future.'

'It's personal, Peter,' was all she could offer in explanation. 'I can't work with or for Steve Rodriguez, and that's all there is to it. I'm truly sorry, believe me, but that's the way it has to be.'

She could raise no enthusiasm for job-hunting, and, since she was in no immediate financial need, decided to leave it for a few weeks. A visit to the family solicitor revealed to her that what remained of the fund set up for Lorraine's medical expenses reverted to her, and there was a considerable amount left.

'I can't think how my stepfather managed to set aside a sum like that, after virtually going bankrupt,' she said, recalling the penny-pinching and the frantic telephone calls for a loan until the end of the month.

The elderly solicitor shook his head.

'I can't help you there, Miss Bradbury. It was all arranged anonymously, through a finance company.' He smiled and essayed a mild joke. 'Perhaps Mr Walton had a win on the horses.'

'Perhaps he did,' Nicole agreed, unable to think of any other explanation.

She lived aimlessly through what remained of the summer, feeling strangely empty. Lorraine's long illness had placed more of a strain on her than she had ever realised at the time—she had not simply died, but had been dying for years—and now that it was over, there was an awful void in Nicole's heart that she did not know how to fill.

But she knew that wasn't all of it. She could not get over the ache caused by her bitter split with Steve, nor kill the memories of him and of the time when he had been part of her life. She told herself that she had to forget him, that she could not forgive what he had done in the past, nor the devious way he had hidden from her his knowledge of who she was, spinning her into his power until that night she still could not drive out of her mind—when he had finally clinched his dominance over her with his careless but absolute possession. But nothing she told herself helped.

Several times a week she made the journey out to Kent, taking flowers to her mother's grave, and she would spend a long time sitting on the short grass of the churchyard, thinking, puzzling, trying to come to terms with the mystery that still eluded her. How *could* he, Steve, the man she had grown to know and love, have behaved in such a way—ever? It did not make sense. But he *had*, and she must accept it. Round and round in her head went the thoughts, a puzzle she would never, ever solve to her own satisfaction.

One afternoon as she sat by the grave, feet tucked under her knees, thoughts far away, Sister Cornelia came upon her.

'Hello, my dear,' she said. 'I'm just on my way to see the vicar.' Her sweet, serene smile spread over her face as she looked down at the girl, whose own expression was so deeply troubled. 'You mustn't grieve too much, Nicole. She wouldn't want you to.'

'I know. I try not to,' Nicole said. 'Most of the time I realise that it's better this way, and I'm so grateful she was spared too much pain.' She frowned. 'Sister, this may sound awful, but it isn't really grief which troubles me. I can accept and cope with that. It's . . . not understanding.'

Sister Cornelia nodded.

'You mean about Mr Rodriguez?' When Nicole's chin jerked up, she went on quietly, 'Oh, my dear, I've sat many hours by your mother's side, often when she was under sedation. They talk, you know. Not that I know the whole story, but his name cropped up again and again, and always spoken with such hate. And that was the man who brought you here the day she died, was it not?'

Noting Nicole's silent assent, she continued.

'He didn't say much, but I've had a lifetime of observing and judging character, and I think I would vouch for the integrity of his. Also for some strong feeling in him for you. Why should a man drop everything to stand by a woman who is merely an employee?'

'If he did have any feeling for me, I've surely killed it,' Nicole said. 'Sister, I don't *know* any more—about anything. All my life I've known that Steve ruined my stepfather, all my life I've hated him—without knowing him. Then I met him, worked for him, lived as part of his family. He's hard, yes, but he's thoughtful, too. He can be very devious and secretive, especially in business, but I've met no one who doesn't swear by his moral uprightness. Yet he refuses to defend or deny what he did. It just doesn't add up!'

Sister Cornelia was quiet for a while, and the breeze whispering through the grass was the only sound.

'Child,' she said finally, 'there are times in all our lives when thinking . . . when reason and knowledge will take us only so far, and we have to listen to the silence inside us. Let your thoughts be quiet for a while, stop allowing them to chase around futilely, getting nowhere. Listen to the truth your own heart is trying to tell you.' She patted Nicole's shoulder. 'I must go. The vicar will be waiting.'

Nicole watched her plump, comfortable shape wend its way across the churchyard towards the vicarage, and alone again with the quiet graves and the whispering grass, she sat utterly still and let her mind clear. And once it was empty of all the bitterness and confusion, something new and sweet and strangely uplifting took possession of it.

She thought of Steve carefully removing the sea urchin spine from her foot, taking her out and making her eat dinner on the traumatic night he caught her in his office. Giving her not just a job, but a promotion, when he could have let her walk out, disgraced. She saw him sheltering her in his arms at the bullfight, when it had been too much for her to take. And she remembered him, last of all, standing firm by her side as they lowered Lorraine into her final resting place.

Steve, who for all his wealth and position still remained friends with the fishermen on the quay. Steve, who ached to be a real father, and had to learn painfully how to go about it. Steve, saying 'nothing is ever quite as it seems', and 'if, after all this time, you still don't know me better than that . . .'

She stood up, feeling the blood return to her cramped limbs, and the exaltation of freedom surge through her along with it.

'I'm sorry, Mother,' she said aloud, 'but I don't believe it! I just don't believe it!'

CHAPTER ELEVEN

MANY times that evening in her flat, Nicole picked up the telephone and put it down again, began to write a letter and then tore it up. What could she say? I think I may have wronged you, but I don't know how? After the awful finality of the way they had parted, and the look in his eyes she could not forget, she did not think he would speak to her or answer any letter she wrote.

The only way to face Steve Rodriguez, as she well knew, was squarely, face to face, with one's courage in both hands. He respected a fighter, however nervous, and had little time for cowards. But Nicole's courage failed her at the thought of confronting those glacial eyes, taking the full scorn of that whiplash tongue. He would probably refuse to see her, anyhow. Nor had she any idea of exactly what it was she wanted to say, or how she would formulate her words. She spent a restless night, and in the morning, unable to bear being confined in the flat, went for a walk in a small park not far away. She walked briskly, stopping at the corner newsagent's for a daily paper to read over her breakfast.

The short item of information was tucked away at the bottom of the foreign page, and it was by the merest of chances it caught her eye. It was not, after all, important news for a British daily, although it could well have made page one in Barcelona or Madrid.

'Bullfighter critically wounded,' she read. 'Matador Miguel Delgado fights for life in hospital after being badly gored in the arena at Barcelona last Sunday.'

Nicole stared at it, cold with horror. Not Miguel, the slim, elegant, unassuming man who had shared *calamares* with them in a restaurant in Figueras? Whose graceful, stylish performance had delighted a crowd of thousands, earlier the same afternoon?

'Oh, no!' she groaned. 'Poor Miguel!' And as the full implications hit her, she added soberly, 'And poor Steve!'

She remembered how he had told her about their long friendship, his visits to the Delgado ranch as a boy—and now, for this to happen, almost at the end of what was to be his friend's final season! This would hit him hard, she knew, and if Miguel were to die . . . Nicole shuddered. It did not bear thinking about.

Unable to rest, she rang the newspaper's foreign desk to try and find out if they had anything further on the story, but no, that was all they knew, and she paced the flat in a frenzy of anxiety, cursing the fact that, eight hundred miles away, Steve was suffering unimaginable torment as his friend fought for survival, and she was in London, powerless to do anything to help him.

She stopped in her tracks. Powerless? This is the twentieth century, girl, she reminded herself. Nowhere is that far from anywhere else, in the jet age. Nowhere in Europe was more than a few flying hours away. He had not hesitated when she had been poleaxed into immobility by Sister Cornelia's emergency call. Putting aside arguments and other business alike, he had got her here in time to be at Lorraine's bedside, whereas, left to her own devices, she might have been far too late. And he had stayed with her, as long as she needed him, until she herself had virtually driven him away. If there was even the faintest possibility that she could offer some help, some comfort, now, what was she waiting for?

Decision spurred her efficiency, blunted by the weeks of inactivity, back into urgent life. She rang round her contacts in the travel trade for the earliest available flight and found a cancellation on a night charter to Gerona, leaving at two-thirty a.m. Summer might be almost at an end in England, but

September was still high season in Spain, and planes were full of holidaymakers. It would have to do. Nicole curbed her impatience by washing her hair, packing a small bag, and doing a thousand unnecessary jobs around the flat, before at last catching the train to the airport.

At Gerona airport, she hired a car, and nervously asked the clerk at the desk if he had heard any more news of the matador who was injured in Barcelona last Sunday. She breathed a heavy sigh of relief on learning that he was still alive, and the clerk gazed after her as she left, surprised by this unexpectedly sympathetic visitor.

The sun rose gloriously as Nicole took the now familiar mountain road, and within half an hour it was so hot she was obliged to stop the car and remove her jacket. She loved this fierce, life-enhancing heat which some found enervating, but which always invigorated her, loved the bare, sunburned hills and the scents of pine and myrtle. How had she persuaded herself she could live without it? she wondered soberly. With the same inane, back-to-front reasoning which had said she could live without Steve? For a moment, her heart almost burst with the sensation of coming home, then she remembered the gravity of the events which had brought her here, and her eyes clouded.

Instinctively she had made for Vistamar. Steve could, she knew, be at the hospital in Barcelona. He could even be at his Figueras apartment, but sooner or later he would return here, to Puerto de Castello, his *'querencia'* as he had once called it. This was where he would come, in trouble or sorrow of any kind, and this was where he would find her waiting. Ready to give whatever he might need in the way of comfort, a listening ear, a hand to hold, or even the willing and unconditional use of her body.

Vistamar was still quiet and shuttered as she turned up the drive. The petals of the roses and pelargoniums looked sculpted in the warm, still air, and there was not a ripple on the shiny azure surface of the pool. It was the loveliest of mornings, promising a day of scorching heat, but for all that the natural world was excelling itself, a pall of gloom lay over the house, and Nicole shivered. Suddenly she felt unwelcome—as if Vistamar were rejecting the compassionate impulse which had brought her here, telling her she had no claim on the emotions of its owner, and that her presence was an intrusion.

Nicole climbed the steps to the front door and pressed the bell lightly, just once. Although it was early, she knew that Dolores would be up. But when the door opened it was Juana, huddled in a white silk robe, her dark hair tousled around her face, who opened it. She looked haggard and tired.

'Nicole,' she said guardedly. 'You're the last person I expected to find at the door.'

'I shall understand if you tell me I'm not wanted,' Nicole said, wondering just how much Steve's sister knew, or had guessed, about their relationship, and about her identity.

She yawned, and then the flicker of a smile illumined her tired face.

'No, come in,' she said. 'Why should you say that?'

Nicole followed her into the lounge, watching her fling open the french windows to admit the already brilliant day.

'I don't know how much Steve told you—about my resignation from the company,' she ventured, and Juana emitted a wry snort.

'Steve, as usual, told me nothing at all, except that you were no longer in his employ, but since he practically bit my head off if I happened to mention you, I gathered there was rather more to it than that,' she said with her usual bluntness. 'Even Lacey gave up on the subject—she went back to the States with Sonia last week, still moaning about your desertion. It might help if you wrote to her.'

'Give me the address and I will,' Nicole promised guiltily. Juana's face softened.

'I'm sorry about your mother,' she said. 'It must have been a blow to you, even though you were expecting it. But I thought you would come back.'

'Well, I'm back now,' Nicole said hastily. Since Steve had kept quiet about her reasons for leaving, she had no desire to go into the subject more deeply right now. 'It's unusual to find you here mid-week, Juana.'

The slim shoulders rose and fell eloquently.

'I know, but I felt I had to be here for Steve—not that I'm being a great deal of use. I don't seem to be able to help him—no one does. See if you can get anywhere.'

The breath faltered in her lungs, as if someone had dealt her a heavy punch.

'He's here at Vistamar—now?' she asked faintly.

'He's here, in body if not in spirit,' Juana confirmed. 'He was at the hospital all day yesterday, giving Miguel's wife what help he could, but now her whole family have turned up, so he came home. I don't think he's slept. He's been in the study all night, waiting for a call from the hospital . . . apparently they aren't sure if Miguel will walk again. I hardly dare ask what the news is.'

Nicole put down her bag and jacket, and touched Juana's arm in a gesture of sympathy.

'I'll go to him,' she said. 'It's what I came for.'

She walked quickly down the corridor to the study, and hesitated for just a second outside the door. Inside was a man who might have received distressing news about his closest friend, and by what right did she, a woman from whom he had parted on harsh terms, presume to think she could help him? But she had not made this impulsive journey in order to stand dithering the wrong side of a door. Setting aside her own fears, she tapped softly and opened it.

The blinds were still partly drawn, and the room was in semi-darkness which temporarily blinded her after the brightness outside, but as her vision adjusted she saw him. He was lying on his back on the leather chesterfield, arms behind is head, absolutely motionless. There was music on the tape deck playing softly . . . a slow, measured beat accompanying a haunting solo guitar, and then the strings coming in afterwards, taking up and intensifying the melody. It was music torn from the soul of Spain, profoundly and unmistakably Iberian.

'Aranjuez Concerto,' the man on the chesterfield said quietly, without moving. And then, 'Why have you come, Nicole?'

The blunt question was discouraging in itself, and there was nothing in his eyes to indicate that her presence gladdened him. But then, how often did those eyes reveal their owner's innermost thoughts?

'I read about the accident in the paper,' she explained. 'I had to come. Is there . . . is there any news about Miguel?'

He swung his legs to the floor and stood up, with the swift, startling fluidity of movement characteristic of him.

'His wife phoned ten minutes ago,' he said. 'The specialist thinks Miguel will have the use of his legs, eventually. The damage to the spinal column is not irreparable. But it will be a long haul.'

Nicole breathed more easily.

'That's good news,' she said. 'Isn't it? After all, he might have died, or been permanently crippled.'

He regarded her with that blank, closed, emotionless expression which had always disturbed her.

'Yes, it's good—or at least, as you observe, it could have been far worse,' he agreed. 'What is it to you, anyway, to bring you all these miles?'

The harshness of this judgement almost robbed her of breath.

'That's a terrible thing to say,' she said quietly. 'All right, so I only met him once, and didn't know him well. But he's your friend, and I could imagine what you must be going through. You were a tower of strength to me when my mother died, and

I don't think I ever thanked you properly. I thought that if there were anything . . . anything at all I could do to make this easier for you . . . then I should be here.'

He was standing no more than a hair's breadth from her, now, so close that she could feel the warmth from his body, so close that her hands itched to reach out and touch him, hold him. But his very stance, erect and unbending, transmitted a wave of cold hostility which froze her in its blast.

'So that's what this mercy dash of yours is all about,' he said, his voice level and chilly. 'Gratitude. You felt you owed me one, did you? Well, save it, Nicole. I don't need your pity and I certainly don't want it. Thank you for your concern, but you need not have troubled.'

She stared at him, afraid that at any moment her knees would start to buckle under her, and her body would concertina to the floor in a useless heap. Stunned by his antagonism, at first she was speechless, and then a small flame sprang into life within her, growing steadily and burning away all the petty feelings of hurt and resentment until all that remained was the pure, strong, unquenchable emotion she had tried for so many months to suppress. The fragile but enduring truth she had finally caught hold of in the quiet churchyard inspired her once again, lending her the strength to say what was really in her heart, whether he had a mind to hear it or not.

'If that's what you think, Steve, then there's nothing I can do about it, and perhaps I can't blame you,' she said softly. 'I didn't come here out of gratitude or pity, or any such notion. I came because I knew you would be hurting, and I wanted to help, if only by sharing your pain. That isn't pity—it's love.'

She paused, licked her dry lips, and hurried on, the words stumbling over one another now, incapable of being held back.

'I want you to know that in spite of what my mother and Teddy told me about what happened all those years ago, in spite of the fact that you refused to deny it when I asked you, I don't believe that you were responsible. Don't ask me to explain why, because I still don't understand it myself. All I can say is that I *know* you, and the man I respect and love just could not have behaved in that way.'

He stood as still, as if her words had turned him to stone, and the silence lengthened between them. Nicole shrugged, and a sense of hopelessness overcome her, driving out the euphoria which had impelled her to speak, as clouds sweep suddenly across a clear sky.

'Well, I think that's about it,' she said, with forced lightness. 'I would say the victory goes to you, Mr Rodriguez.'

Aranjuez flooded the room, filling it with a soaring, bitter-sweet passion as Nicole closed the door quietly behind her. Then her composure deserted her all at once, and in sudden distress she ran down the corridor, past a startled Juana, who was unable to restrain her, and out of the front door on to the terrace. Her car stood waiting on the drive, but the keys were in her bag in the hall, and nothing, at that moment, would have induced her to go back into that house where she had just left her heart bleeding and rejected in the dust.

Turning her back on the drive, she ran past the swimming pool, through the gardens and, seeking nothing but escape and solitude, out through the rear gate behind the tennis court, into the blessed anonymity of the wooded hills. A dusty path led upwards through the forest, and Nicole followed it, climbing and scrambling until she was out of breath, and Vistamar was far below her. She gasped for air, and then blindly went on climbing, like a hunted and panic-stricken animal, tears and perspiration mingling to stream down her face.

The truth she had come by so hard, agonised over so deeply, the injustice she believed she had done him, and wanted so badly to put right—he had been totally unmoved by either. Her love had left him cold, but why had she ever thought it would matter to him how she felt? She'd done the only thing she could, she'd set the record straight, and now there was nothing left for her here. It was over.

Nicole did not know how long she climbed the steep path up the hillside, but after a while, brushing away her tears with her equally damp hand, she saw that she was no longer in the forest but among cultivated vineyards either side of the path, which had broadened out. There were people at work among the vines, and they smiled and waved at her as she passed. No one challenged her right to use the path, which was obviously well trodden and leading somewhere—not that she cared, in her wretched state, if it led stright to hell. It was not possible to imagine she could feel more dejected and unhappy than this, no matter where she went, or what she did.

Hot, dusty, the sun beating down on her unprotected head and bare arms, she stumbled past a farmhouse, then more scattered dwellings, and glancing up, she saw the ruined castle dead ahead on the skyline. The path, as she now remembered from wandering these hills long ago, was a back route through the vineyards to the village of San Martín de Castello, where she and Steve had lunched on that memorable and now long-ago-seeming day when he took her to the corrida at Figueras.

Nicole emerged from a tiny back street into the square and collapsed thankfully into a cane chair outside one of the restaurants, hoping the few *pesetas* in the pocket of her dress would be sufficient to pay for a cool drink. She was the only customer. It was too early for the tourists, and the locals were all busy in the fields, or about their respective business. She leaned back, closing her eyes. Her head throbbed painfully from her injudicious exposure to the sun, and her throat was parched with thirst, but neither drove out the deep ache lodged firmly beneath her heart.

She knew someone was standing by the table in front of her, because their presence blocked out the sun and created a patch of cool shadow. She opened her eyes, expecting to see the waiter, but it was Steve's uncle, Enrique Rodriguez, who looked down at her. His smile was gentle and, unlike the day she had last seen him, his eyes were clear and unconfused.

'*Bon día, señorita.*' He addressed her in the local dialect. 'I believe we have met. My nephew, Esteban, brought you here one day.'

This polite elderly gentleman seemed totally different from the bewildered old man who had mistaken her for Sonia. 'He has periods of remarkable clarity,' Steve had said, and no one meeting him today would suspect that he suffered from a degenerative and incurable condition.

'That's right—I'm Nicole Bradbury.' She hoped her face was not too streaky and tear-stained, for he was regarding her with a gentle concern. 'I'm a bit out of breath, I'm afraid. I walked up through the vineyards, and it's very hot.'

He eased his large frame into the chair beside her, and clicked his fingers for the waiter in an authoritative gesture which reminded her of Steve.

'Bradbury,' he said thoughtfully, rolling the word around on his tongue. Nicole had introduced herself unthinkingly, for it never occurred to her that the name would mean anything to him. He was silent as his thick black coffee and her lemonade were placed on the table before them, and then he startled her by adding, 'Teddy Walton was married to a woman called Bradbury . . . *Lorraine* Bradbury, her name was. Any relation?'

Nicole took a gulp of her drink, swallowing it more quickly than she had intended, and coughed.

'My mother,' she said quickly. 'She died . . . a few weeks ago.'

He peered at her more closely.

'I remember *you,*' he said suddenly, 'although I would never have recognised you. Quiet little thing, you were—always wandering about on your own. I'm sorry to hear about your mother. Teddy's dead, too, I suppose.'

There was a constricted sensation in Nicole's throat which impared her breathing and made her have to struggle for speech. This was like taking a journey back into her own past, and conversing with ghosts.

'Yes. He died some years ago,' she told him.

He sniffed imperturbably and sipped his coffee.

'I can't say I'm surprised. He lived too fast to survive to any great age, did Teddy. *Que loco!* Silly old fool,' he said, in a tone of affectionate criticism.

'He . . . wasn't very happy in his last few years,' Nicole defended her stepfather carefully. 'We had lost everything . . . he didn't feel there was much to live for.'

'Ah.' Enrique Rodriguez sighed, and shrugged philosophically. 'Well, he brought that on himself, didn't he, when he started stealing from the business? Shouldn't have done it.'

Nicole sat straight upright, her exhaustion gone, every nerve alert and straining. Did he know what he was saying? She stared into the face of Steve's uncle, searching for a shadow of doubt, a trace of confusion. But she found none. This was a man in total recall of the past, talking candidly of events as they had happened, and people as they had been.

'*Teddy* stole from the business?' she repeated slowly, this new and revolutionary idea taking time to sink its full implications into her mind.

'Didn't you know that? I didn't grasp what was happening, myself, for a long time,' the old man reminisced. 'I'm a practical man, you see, no good at figures, and he did it very cleverly. But I knew we were losing money, lots of it, and it had to stop. I got young Esteban over from America. He sorted it out, although I never knew how he did it. I was ill after that, very ill. I didn't want to think it was Teddy, but . . .' a flicker of pain crossed his face '. . . I think I knew that it had to be.'

In the voice and the manner of this old man, with nothing to lose or gain, now, from what he told her, Nicole heard for the first time the unmistakable ring of truth. Teddy, her mother's beloved companion, the man who had been like a father to her, must have lied to them both about his part in this murky business. He had not been the injured party at all, but the wrongdoer, and if that were true, it followed automatically that Steve was innocent of the misdeeds she had been brought up believing him to have committed.

Which was no more than what she had come to believe herself, against all the evidence in her possession—what Sister Cornelia had called the truth her own heart was trying to tell her. But why hadn't Steve told her of all this when she gave him the opportunity, and spared her so much anguish and bewilderment—to say nothing of clearing his own name?

The door to the tall old house opposite flew open, and the nurse bustled across to them.

'Señor Rodriguez!' she reprimanded him sternly. 'That was very naughty of you, to slip out without telling me!' She took his arm. 'Come along now—it's time for your medication.'

'Oh, hold your tongue, woman,' he retorted mildly. 'This beautiful young lady is better medication than anything you have to offer!' He leaned across to Nicole and said, 'Have to keep them in their place, you know! Get Esteban to bring you again some time and we'll talk some more.'

But he submitted cheerfully to the nurse's orders, and Nicole watched helplessly as he allowed himself to be led back inside. So much knowledge of those days was locked up inside his head, and if they talked a thousand times, she knew she might never again find him as clear and in possession of his mental faculties as she had today.

Nicole left the café table and walked slowly through the village, and up the hill towards the crumbling ruins of the old castle. Here, in the shade of a broken wall, she sat down, hands clasped around her knees, chin resting on them, gazing thoughtfully into the distances. From this height it was posible to look clear over the rooftops of San Martín, the vineyards and hills beyond, and catch a glimpse of the sparkling sea and the rocky convolutions of the coast. But Nicole regarded it all unseeingly.

It was hard to learn at the age of twenty-four that a man you had loved as a father, whose word you had trusted, was an embezzler who had blamed another man for his misdemeanours. It hurt, because she still loved Teddy, and could not switch off all those years of loving, in spite of what he had done. But, beneath the pain of this betrayal, her heart sang with vindication of the trust she had come by so hard. She had not fallen in love with a cheat and a swindler. She had loved Steve, whose only crime had been to protect the interests of his family, and, even if it no longer made any difference to the outcome, she was proud to have loved him. Nicole lowered her forehead to her clasped hands and began to cry helplesly, unable to stem the flow, but this time there was relief mingled with the pain.

She never heard him approach, and when he dropped to the grass beside her, she looked up, startled, into his face, which was gentle now. In fact, he was smiling very faintly.

'Is all this for my benefit?' he asked softly. 'Please don't. Traditionally, I should have a handkerchief, but all I've got is a box of tissues, and they're in the glove compartment of the car. Will my shirt do? It *is* clean.'

Through her tears, Nicole felt the onset of a half-hysterical laughter.

'Steve, stop it!' she begged. 'I feel foolish enough as it is! However did you track me here?'

'Not difficult,' he pointed out. 'I watched you climb the path behind the house from the study window. But I thought so much exertion might be bad for me, at my age, so I got the car out and drove round by the road. The waiter at the café pointed me in this direction.'

The teasing note vanished from his voice, and his face was intent as he looked at her.

'You left your handbag and your jacket behind you—also a bombshell which you flung at my feet before your headlong flight,' he told her. 'You referred to me as the man you loved.

Was that intended, or a slip of the tongue?'

'It wasn't a slip of anything,' she protested, and, as she had longed to do all those weeks without him, she reached up and touched his face with wondering fingers. Turning his head, he seared the back of her hand with a long kiss, and lowered her to the springy, sweet-smelling grass, his mouth finding hers, his hands moving over her body in a light but urgent journey of rediscovery.

Already, her senses had begun to swim with the release of long-suppressed desire. She had no words worth saying, no questions which must be answered, as important as loving him here, now, this minute, feeling him close to her, inside her, and enveloping her body with his. It was ten o'clock on a bright morning on a Spanish hillside, with only the old, ruined castle, open to the sky, to offer them privacy, but he was already dealing with the zipper of her dress, and she sensed in him a determined and impatient passion her own need leapt to meet.

'Only eagles and hang-gliders can see us up here, my love,' he said softly, and then there was nothing but the silken seduction of his flesh against hers, taking her swiftly and urgently, as she wanted to be taken. No time now for slow dalliance, only an imperative, insistent need to claim and be claimed. She cried out once, as her pleasure reached its peak, and the sky and earth all around them dissolved into a hazy limbo, and then she subsided in his arms.

'We must be crazy!' she gasped as they leaned against the sun-warmed stone of the wall behind them, still slightly dishevelled, but dressed and respectable once more. 'Anyone could have walked in on us!'

'Everyone knows what happens to English girls once they are let loose in Spain,' he grinned. 'They would only think you were running true to form.'

'That would have been my excuse—what's yours?' she retorted. 'A respected pillar of the community, disporting himself in the grass with a woman, in broad daylight! Your image would never recover.'

'I'd plead that you took me by storm,' he said, adding half seriously, 'You did, in a sense, the first time we made love. I hadn't expected such instant compatibility, such complete perfection. And if I was hard on you, it was because I didn't really enjoy being desired in spite of my villainy. I wanted a love based on trust.'

Nicole digested this quietly for a while.

'You said I threw a bombshell at your feet this morning. In fact, I just had one tossed into my lap,' she said. 'I was talking to your uncle Enrique—he's as lucid as you or I today—and he told me that Teddy was embezzling from the company. If that's true, Steve—and I've accepted that it must be—why didn't you tell me?'

Steve let out a sigh of incredulity and, turning away from her, lowered his head to his hands. He was silent for some minutes, and she did not press him further. She had learned at last to know that inward-turned response to strong, concealed emotion. At last, he straightened up and looked her directly in the eyes.

'That's ironic,' he said. 'I've tried, all these years, to keep it from him that his old friend had played dirty tricks on him. I never told him, we never spoke about it. But, somewhere in the part of his mind that occasionally functions clearly, he must have always known.'

'Don't you think it's about time you told me the whole of it?' Nicole asked gently, and he smiled his acknowledgment.

'Since you already know the gist, and my uncle does too, then I suppose I must,' he admitted. 'It will be a relief, in a way.'

He took a deep breath and spoke quietly, expressionlessly, keeping the story as factual and free of emotion as he could.

'I came back from America ten years ago because my uncle sent an SOS saying the family business was in dire trouble, and could I help find out why? Naturally, I agreed. I had planned all along to come back to Spain, and my marriage was already in trouble, so I didn't have a lot to lose.'

He gave a slight shrug.

'My father's insistence on a degree in business methods paid off. It didn't take me too long to discover that someone had been gradually and cunningly draining funds away, or to pinpoint the culprit.'

It was Nicole's turn to sigh.

'But why, Steve? Teddy was so kind, so sweet . . . he wasn't the sort of man who sets out in life to defraud his friends.'

'No, and listen, Nicole, I don't want you to swing to the other extreme and start blaming him, as all these years you have blamed *me*,' he said soberly. 'Teddy loved you and your mother very much, never doubt that. He wanted you to have everything money could provide, and so he over-extended himself. Loans all over the place, credit he couldn't keep up with, a house he couldn't really afford. He began taking money from the company, a little at a time, to keep himself afloat, and then, as these things do, it snowballed. He was in way over his head, and the company was well on its way to going broke I only just managed to turn it round.'

'I understand that,' Nicole said. 'But why the secrecy?'

'I'm coming to that. Teddy came to see me in great distress. Far worse than the prospect of being bankrupt, he feared losing the love and esteem of his wife and his daughter. He offered to give up his share in the business, Vistamar, and everything he had, if only he could be spared that. I agreed to what he asked. It was quicker than dragging the whole thing through the courts, and I was anxious to start getting the business back on its feet.'

'But it was your good name that was spoilt,' Nicole pointed out. 'You let him off lightly—he could have been sent to prison —and in return, he defamed you thoroughly. And you never defended yourself even to me.'

'I gave him my word I would never reveal what had happened,' he said. 'My word has to be my bond, Nicole, or it's useless. Even when Teddy died, there was still Lorraine, who treasured her husband's memory, and *Tío* Enrique, whom I did not want to hurt. As for anyone else, I had to trust that anyone who really knew me would disregard the rumours.'

'Oh, Steve—your word to a man who is senile, and another who is dead, whose wife hated you right to her last moments!' Nicole shook her head, thinking, horrified, how very close she had come to going on believing this myth, and letting it ruin her life. 'You would never have told me, if I hadn't found out—would you?'

'No, I never would,' he agreed. 'I couldn't—don't you see? It had all ceased to be important until you came back to Spain, spitting hatred at me like an angry, bristling little cat, and never letting on who you were.'

'I was afraid to,' she admitted. 'My mother had warned me so often about you, I thought of you as the devil incarnate.'

'You made that very clear. At first I thought you had malice in mind, so I kept a close watch on you . . . and then, my darling, I began not only to be attracted to you, but to want your good opinion, to care what you thought, which is why I insisted you work for me and live at Vistamar. I couldn't just let you go, and I thought if you got to know me you would come to understand what a regular good guy I was!' he joked.

And then he fell serious again.

'I believe that a strong enough truth must become self-evident, and you would come to know it for yourself, without my having to break my word to tell you. I loved you, and believed that if you loved me, your own instincts would tell you I wasn't guilty.'

She leaned her head against his shoulder.

'So they did—but it was a close thing!' she shuddered. 'You took a huge gamble there!'

'No, my love, merely a calculated risk,' he contradicted. 'I wanted all of you—or nothing. An unwilling, guilty love would have been no good to me. If I'm going to take a second plunge into matrimony, I have to be very, very sure.'

The blue eyes were full of delighted laughter as they gazed into his.

'Aren't you taking rather a lot for granted?' she asked teasingly.

'Am I? No, I don't think so. Why should you turn me down? I'm rich, handsome, and crazy about you.'

'And conceited with it,' she murmured.

'As you say,' he conceded with a smile. 'Let's go and break the news to Juana—she'll be delighted to have you for a sister-in-law. Then we'll put a call through to the States and make Lacey's day.'

He pulled her to her feet, gripping her hands with a hard, firm pressure which told her he had no intention of ever letting her go again. Still riding the crest of an ecstatic wave, Nicole paused, holding him back when he would have hurried ahead to the waiting celebrations.

'There's still one thing which puzzles me about Teddy,' she said.

Steve shrugged impatiently.

'Forget Teddy—forgive him for his foolishness, then let it go. It's all in the past,' he urged her. 'He paid dearly enough for what he did, by losing everything.'

'But that's just it,' Nicole said slowly. 'He *didn't* lose it all, or where did the money come from to help me through university, and pay for the nursing home? And there's still a large sum left in the bank.'

She stared into the grey eyes which held hers, unrevealing as ever, but she had learned to search beyond that façade, and as she achieved a close and intimate contact with the mind which was no longer a stranger to her, the last of the mystery dropped away, leaving her free and clear in the sunlight of understanding.

'It was you!' she said. 'That money came from you, didn't it? You kept tabs on us, all those years! The anonymous fund, paid through the bank . . . neatly tied up so that Teddy couldn't get his hands on it first!'

He shrugged again, and for the first time she sensed a certain embarrassment in him.

'Don't make a big deal out of it, Nicole,' he said. 'You and Lorraine were innocents—I merely didn't see why you should suffer.'

'But it must have been hard for you to spare that money, at first, when you still had to rebuild the company,' she persisted.

He draped an arm round her shoulder.

'I'm a businessman, I thrive on challenge,' he told her. 'All in all, I think I made a pretty shrewd investment, don't you? Look what I got by way of return. She's beautiful, she's incredibly sexy, and on top of all that, she has brains! Not only do I get a mother for my children, I get a potential board member, too!'

Nicole slid her arms round him and rested her head against his chest, savouring the warm beat of his heart under her cheek.

'Which of those projects would you like me to work on first—partner?'

'What do *you* think?' he replied, laughing. And, arms still tight around each other's waist, they made their way back down the hill towards the brightly shining future that beckoned.

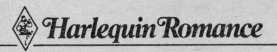
Harlequin Romance

Coming Next Month

Available in March wherever paperback books are sold, or
through Harlequin Reader Service:

In the U.S.   In Canada
901 Fuhrmann Blvd.   P.O. Box 603
P.O. Box 1397   Fort Erie, Ontario
Buffalo, N.Y. 14240-1397   L2A 5X3

ATTRACTIVE, SPACE SAVING BOOK RACK

Display your most prized novels on this handsome and sturdy book rack. The hand-rubbed walnut finish will blend into your library decor with quiet elegance, providing a practical organizer for your favorite hard-or soft-covered books.

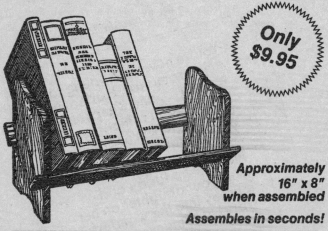

Only $9.95

**Approximately
16" x 8"
when assembled**

Assembles in seconds!

To order, rush your name, address and zip code, along with a check or money order for $10.70* ($9.95 plus 75¢ postage and handling) payable to *Harlequin Reader Service*:

Harlequin Reader Service
Book Rack Offer
901 Fuhrmann Blvd.
P.O. Box 1396
Buffalo, NY 14269-1396

Offer not available in Canada.

*New York and Iowa residents add appropriate sales tax.

BKR-1A

Keepsake